I0831522

At the Café

and

The Talisman

CARAF Books
Caribbean and African Literature Translated from French

Carrol F. Coates, Editor

Clarisse Zimra, J. Michael Dash,
and Elisabeth Mudimbe-Boyi,
Advisory Editors

MOHAMMED DIB

At the Café & The Talisman

Translated by C. Dickson

Afterword by Mildred Mortimer

UNIVERSITY OF VIRGINIA PRESS CHARLOTTESVILLE AND LONDON

Ouvrage publié avec le soutien du Centre national du livre—
ministère français chargé de la culture.

Publication of this translation was assisted by a grant from the French Ministry of Culture, National Center of the Book.

Originally published in French as *Au café, nouvelles* (Paris: Gallimard, 1955) and reprinted by Sindbad, 1984, and *Le talisman, nouvelles* (Paris: Éditions du Seuil, 1966),

University of Virginia Press

First published 2011

9 8 7 6 5 4 3 2 1

LIBRARY OF CONGRESS CATALOGING-IN-PUBLICATION DATA
Dib, Mohammed, 1920–2003.
[Short stories. English. Selections]
At the cafe ; and, The talisman / Mohammed Dib ; translated by C. Dickson ; afterword by Mildred P. Mortimer.
p. cm. — (CARAF books: Caribbean and African literature translated from French)
Includes bibliographical references.
ISBN 978-0-8139-3119-7 (cloth : alk. paper) — ISBN 978-0-8139-3120-3 (pbk. : alk. paper) — ISBN 978-0-8139-3147-0 (ebk.)
1. Dib, Mohammed, 1920–2003—Translations into English. I. Dickson, C. II. Dib, Mohammed, 1920–2003. Au Café. English. III. Dib, Mohammed, 1920–2003. Talisman. English. IV. Title.
PQ3989.D52A2 2011
843'.914—dc22 2010045464

CONTENTS

At the Café

AT THE CAFÉ

It was late; I was wondering if I shouldn't be leaving the noisy, dark café. Sitting alone at a table, I was observing groups of people around me who were talking and smoking nonstop. In the dim background, players slammed down their dominoes with sharp whiplike snaps that wore on one's nerves in the long run. The walls were covered with dirty smudges and, higher up, the dark yellow plaster grew ever filthier until it reached the soot-blackened ceiling. Against the walls were long, wide wooden benches that could hold as many as ten people, while old dusty straw-seated chairs were strewn about in the middle of the room. A dense cloud of smoke hovered over everything and slowly dissipated into a diffuse, acrid vapor in the white glow of the lightbulbs.

I was watching the door, chained to the bench with an odd feeling of torpor. Through the windows, the sky was leaden and morose. With a faint uninterrupted howling sound, the wind was shaking the tall trees of place du Beylick as it melted slowly into the darkness. I could no longer muster the strength to leave.

I sank further back into my corner; a deep, all-encompassing feeling of inner well-being, a nagging uncertainty, filled my heart and I couldn't stop thinking of the hostile rainy night blanketing the city. In the café, amid the smoky blur of the teeming crowd, I was at least sheltered and could savor that pleasant sensation of warmth.

There was nothing but a bunch of poor wretches in there, homeless men and uprooted fellahs who had deserted the fields and who could be recognized from their sharp, leathered, deeply furrowed features. They all exuded the same aura of indigence. Each of the people hanging around there was as useless and unstable as any one of those chairs. With the exception, however, of a well-groomed, clean little man all bundled up in a white wool djellaba, whose presence seemed astonishingly out of place in that hole-in-the-wall filled with a mixture of worn clothing, greasy fezes, ragged burnooses and cloaks.

Like most of the people, I was there to while away the hours. Though I knew my children were waiting for me, my wife was waiting for me. What do you expect! I hadn't brought them anything to eat for several days, not a cent had fallen into my pocket for several days. So I preferred to stay at the café.

It was raining; night had fallen long ago. The wind was blowing in icy gusts and I was hunched up in my corner, numbed, trying to forget everything except the pleasant warmth that had crept into my body. I was huddling over myself to hold it in, while the hectic café life seethed all around. Patiently, I too was waiting; I was waiting for fatigue to overwhelm my children, close their eyes, which asked the mute and dreadful question, always that same question, as soon as they saw me come home. I was waiting for sleep to loosen their poor emaciated limbs, lay upon their little gray faces, as if covered with ashes, an expression of repose at last. I was waiting for my wife, weary of waiting up, to go to bed. I was waiting.

Outside, darkness, cold, penetrating humidity. The wailing of the wind grew more deafening and, from time to time, the rain would suddenly pelt down harder on the Beylick shacks that could be vaguely distinguished leaning up against one another. My heart clung to the sensation of reassuring warmth I felt in that café, with my feet all nice and dry. And yet the small fire burning within me continued to slowly die out. I examined the shadows through the misty windows again. Suddenly, I shivered.

"This has been going on for three years now," I thought, and gazed out into the darkness. "I've been living in fear of going home, for three years." At that same instant, I thought I saw a hideous face with an enigmatic, bleak grimace staring at me.

The persistent swoosh of invisible raindrops falling brought sad thoughts to my mind. Undoubtedly my restless, exacerbated imagination was distracting itself by setting those perverse fantasies, those strange make-believe visions before my eyes. In any event, while the rain beat down on the roofs of the shacks, while the wind whistled with a worried and plaintive note, and monotonous, desperate blasts gusted, a feeling of unbearable tedium—of such lassitude it was nauseating—crept over me, a feeling that made me want to flee, the devil knows where.

While my eyes were riveted on the door and morose thoughts were rolling around in my mind, I was still torn between the desire to leave and the irresistible need to prolong this respite a few more minutes when, pushing one of the swinging doors timidly open, as if he barely had enough strength, a man slipped into the café. For God's sake! A man of that size coming in on his tiptoes! Once through the door, he stood still. He looked around with terribly vacant eyes, staring intently at the room, the people, the walls; I was disturbed by the look in his eyes.

In the overly hot atmosphere of the café he must have immediately felt a sensation of well-being; his shoulders, which had been drawn up around his ears, slowly relaxed. The man was tall, deep-chested; he seemed to be about forty years of age, even more. But how could it be that his beard was completely gray? If it hadn't been for his European suit, with that beard, I would have taken him for a member of the Derkaoua sect.* To go with the beard, he had a thin handsome face, one of those faces with a noble, gentle air about it, marked nevertheless with a certain severity, even sadness, which one often finds in peasants who live very near the city.

He was blinking a little, his eyes stinging with the smoke or the sudden glare of the bare electric lightbulbs hanging like pears from their wires. From all sides, gray curls of smoke roiled through the heavy air of the room. An indescribable commotion of voices, interspersed with cries, with calls, indis-

*Disciples of Sheik Derkaoui, who have special mystical practices; organized into a powerful sect, these followers have played, at different times, an important role in politics.

tinct chatter, laughter, rose incessantly, as in a sort of collective, confused, and earsplitting hysteria.

The expression on the man's face was just as odd as the look in his eyes: you would have thought he came from a distant land, that he wasn't familiar with the language and the customs of the men around him, and that was why he merely stood there contemplating people and things in that way, with no hope of communicating.

"After all," I said to myself, "it's undoubtedly some poor devil who's come in to beg in spite of the time." Not being used to doing so, he probably didn't dare hold out his hand. And maybe he also wanted to take advantage of the salutary effect of the warmth, before going back out into the inclement night.

As I was reflecting in that way, I noticed all the same that he didn't look like a beggar or a vagabond: his brown woolen suit was not new, but was still quite proper and looked, I must admit, better than my own; the shoes he was wearing also seemed to be in good condition.

Then, as if he'd grown braver, he started walking toward the tables. His curious gaze was now fixed on me; he was walking in my direction with cautious, quiet steps. Coming up to my table, he leaned over and carefully pulled out one of the small benches there and sat down without further ado.

"May God come to your aid," he said as a greeting.

His voice was ordinary, but there was a sort of veil over it which made it sound muffled. He put an elbow on the table, avoiding the dark spills in places. The wooden table wobbled under the weight. He took his elbow off and laid his hands on his knees, straightening his torso. His eyes remained pinned on me the whole time. Now that he was closer, I could see that despite his holding them open so widely, there was something dreamy about his bluish-gray eyes under the bristling brows. Examined in that way, at close range, they lost their disconcerting fixedness. The man at my table remained silent for quite some time.

Already forgetting his presence, I drifted back into my thoughts. I was imagining the pale little sharp-angled faces of my children sleeping, having lost all hope of seeing me come home. The man beside me coughed slightly, with a special kind of cough. Then I realized he wanted to talk to me.

"Brother, I've just been released from prison," he informed me in his muffled voice.

It came as a revelation to me: how could I not have realized that before? Everything about him pointed to it. The slippery, silent look, the docile way of moving, the eyes that seemed to suck everything up, the steady, muted voice . . . Of course! All of that eloquently described a man who had spent a long time, maybe years, behind the thick walls of the civilian prison. Why hadn't I guessed it before?

A worrisome thought suddenly came to me. This man had obviously come up to me in order to ask for some kind of help, some meager fare at the least. Whereas, in the bottom of my pocket, all I had were the few francs with which I intended to pay for the tea I had drunk a couple of hours earlier. The glass had even disappeared from the table, whisked away by the waiter. He knew his clients and felt it unnecessary to leave the glasses until he had been paid.

I looked at my companion. Knowing that I could be of no assistance, I was getting ready to turn my back on him, even show my hostility toward him, in order to quell any urge he might have to carry the conversation any further. Then I felt ashamed of myself. So I darted encouraging glances at him. I was on the verge of asking him what had led him to be imprisoned, but refrained in time.

I don't know why, but suddenly I saw myself in Paris long ago when—filled with illusions—I had gone there believing, like so many of my countrymen, I would find work easily. I had just arrived. Luckily, I had taken certain precautions: I had brought along all my savings, a tidy little sum, if I do say so myself, which would allow me to live comfortably for at least two months in the city of Paris, to which I was still a stranger. One day, I was walking down a small street when a Frenchman came up to me; he was short-legged, fat, with an egg-shaped head covered with a woolly red mane that was so frizzy you would have thought his hair had been recently singed in a fire. He was holding out two yellow metro tickets. I noticed the look in his eyes immediately. It was exactly like that of the man sitting before me then in the café.

The redhead said, "Sir, would you like to buy these tickets? I've just been released from prison and I haven't a cent."

Without saying a word, I took the money from the right pocket of my suit jacket, where I kept some small bills and change for my daily expenses. I put the money in his hand and, stupidly, accepted the metro tickets. But when I changed my mind and tried to call him back so I could return those pathetic tickets, he had already disappeared.

That had been quite some time ago. I later found myself back in Algeria, and once again out of work . . . but let's not talk about that!

Sitting there facing the man, I was beginning to ask myself if there really wasn't some mysterious sign that singled me out to people of this sort, drew them to me.

I questioned the man, "How long did you spend in prison?"

"Five years," he answered in a calm voice.

I admit that an absurd thought crossed my mind just then. "I've been looking for work for three years now, and this man hasn't experienced the slightest difficulty for five whole years." That was when I became curious to learn how he had ended up in that situation.

I remarked that my interest in him was mixed with a budding feeling of friendship. I had never felt afraid of any man, no matter who he was. Generally speaking, even a murderer is not irrevocably lost. With people like that, who are considered to be the dregs of society, the thing we need to fear most is precisely meting out too heavy a punishment, which could well extinguish the human spark in them, kill aspirations of generosity in their hearts and turn them into ferocious beasts. But I felt there was something altogether different about this stranger, something exciting and unusual.

I glanced at him. His eyes were closed. He truly did have a handsome face; the gray beard of equal growth over his face, curling at the ends, suited him admirably well and lent him an air of spirituality that was impossible to explain. When he opened his eyes after a second, he was gazing at me with a gentle, pained expression. I was taken aback: my curiosity gave way to a feeling that was completely new to me and quite unpleasant.

To break the silence, and above all to drive out the uneasy feeling I was having, I uttered the first words that came to mind.

"I beg your pardon, I would so like to offer you a glass of tea, but I have no money. Other than this, to pay for the tea I already drank."

I showed him the coins in the palm of my hand, which I had fished out of one of my pockets, mingled in with fluff balls, gray bread crumbs, and bits of tobacco.

"What?" he said, raising his eyebrows very high, looking surprised. "Not at all! I'll be the one who's paying. Please excuse me for not having mentioned it, I didn't think you wanted to drink anything . . ."

I was about to answer that it had nothing to do with me, but he had already called the waiter. When he asked the young man to bring us a large teapot, the waiter seemed astonished at the unexpected order. He was on the verge of saying, what?—or something or other—but went off without having opened his mouth.

"Hey," said my host, "why not? The occasion calls for it, don't you agree? One doesn't get out of prison every day."

He fell silent and didn't say another word until the teapot was set down on the table between us.

He went on, "I earned some money in there, because they made us work. When I left, they gave it all to me."

Taking hold of the teapot, he went about the task of filling our glasses. "I don't know anyone here. May I?"

But in spite of this conversation, I sensed he wasn't the kind to waste energy on small talk. His sentences were brief and not always very clear either.

Then I said things to him I would never have thought myself capable of saying to a stranger, "You have a kind face . . ."

I could no longer stop myself and added, "You don't look like a . . . murderer."

Turning toward me resolutely, he sat squarely on his bench,

leaning his hands on his knees, and in one breath words poured from his mouth.

"You think that I killed a man, brother? That I'm a savage beast? No, I'm not what you think."

He spoke in that manner for a long time, without stopping, closing his eyes often. He spoke slowly, in a clear but low voice; the movement of his lips enhanced their firm outline. I wish I could remember everything he said. There was something extraordinary about the tone of his voice. The look in his eyes was also exceptional. Yet the stranger spoke calmly, in a way men never speak about themselves.

From that moment on, I began to lose confidence in myself. All the ideas I had thought firmly based abandoned me. That man, of whose very existence I had been unaware only a half-hour ago, through his words, through the look in his eyes, had just turned everything I was familiar with upside down and laid bare the lie—yes, I dare to say it now, the lie—of the world, the hypocritical satisfaction with which life is veneered, encrusted. Thus, deep down inside, I—who had known nothing but setbacks until then—put up with it, I accepted it all. But why? Simply because I believed everything would turn out all right in the end, I simply needed to be patient. "Once I get a good grip on life," I would say to console myself, "I'll show them what I'm capable of." But in the meantime, blinded by the fallacious feeling of security, I was losing my footing a little more each day, I was going further and further adrift . . .

I revealed none of my inner turmoil to the stranger, but he must have gotten some hint of it.

This is the story he related.

The man had not intended to kill, but simply to steal. It was the first time he had ever stolen anything. From what I was able to understand, his act had been spurred by hunger, idleness, and unbearable boredom; all were eating away at him at once. The incident took place under the following circumstances: one night as he was wandering around, jobless, he happened upon a small cart hauling large cardboard boxes back from the train station. He slipped behind the vehicle, slit open one of the boxes easily with his pocket knife. The driver was walking up front beside his horse, having no idea what was going on in back.

"I didn't know what I was going to find," remarked my tablemate. "But it was biscuits! What a windfall, wouldn't you say, brother? They were for the distinguished people of the city. 'Well!' I said to myself, 'I'll have my share too.'"

He dug in with both hands, filled his pockets, slipped some under his shirt. The driver noticed and pounced upon him. My man struck him in the temple with his fist. The other fell.

"I looked at him," he said. "He remained lying at my feet, with his face turned toward me, eyes bulging, mouth agape. Suddenly, I was dumbstruck. I bent over and tried to lift his head: it was as heavy as a butcher block and fell from my hands to one side and then to the other. There was still the angry glare in his eyes, but it was already turning to a terrifyingly cold, stony gaze. Then I felt the blood oozing from his skull and covering my hands. In the meantime, the little cart was rolling away on its own, pulled along by the blinkered steed. All at once I began screaming like a madman, 'Hey! Good people, I've killed a man!'"

Little time went by between the swift, brutal tragedy and the moment when he was taken to the police station and later imprisoned.

As he spoke, he gazed straight ahead. Although his pale eyes did not move, I thought I caught sight of the faint glimmer of dread that comes over people who suddenly come face-to-face with their destiny. Without realizing what he was doing, he had joined his hands, and was clenching them together, wringing them so hard the bones were cracking.

"In prison," he went on, "surrounded by thieves and criminals, I lived as if in a fog. I didn't understand what was happening to me anymore; the thoughts that came to my mind filled my soul with terror. At night I believed I could hear the inmates moving next to me and my hair would stand on end. I lived in that state of mind for a long time; I wasn't able to sleep anymore, wasn't able to partake of the daily fare I was given, it remained untouched. I could only concentrate on the thoughts that kept cropping up, kept proliferating in my mind.

But what? What's gone wrong here? I would endlessly ask myself; a man breathes, goes about his business; I come along, I hit him on the head—and he no longer exists! What do you say about that? What is life then? God created him, and I killed him. Therefore, I felt no pity for his soul, for his business, his miserable existence, the sweat of his brow, or the woman who had brought him into this world . . . It is as if someone had given me a sheep and said to me: cut its throat. He was my equal and I killed him as if he were an animal.

"After that, I got out of prison, but it's as if I were still asleep; I understand even less of what is going on in the world. I can see people walking around all right, coming and going; they gesticulate, talk, buy, sell, work, build; some run around, others take it easy, dragging their feet; some pass by in automobiles, and most on foot. But none of them have an inkling of what is going on in my mind. 'I'm going to start looking for work,' I say to myself. 'I'll go asking around everywhere. I'll be tempted to steal again if I don't find work. When one gets too hungry . . .' Once again, strange thoughts are on the prowl. 'I could kill again—*anyone*,' someone whispers in my head. Or, '*Anyone could kill me* . . . !' Consequently, it seems to me that the world is draining away, growing ever emptier; all that is left of the crowd around me is an army of intangible, fleeting shadows."

After that, he spoke of human weakness; his ascetic face darkened, took on inspired beauty. Unfortunately, his eyes were lit with a sinister madness, and the words he used were overwrought, as if stemming from delirium.

"In prison, I was withdrawn, always silent, avoiding the other prisoners. They would ask me, 'Hey you! Why are you always so sad? Have you lost someone? Are you in mourning?' It was indeed a question of having lost someone! I was mourning over the human race, the way of the world. Ah, that wonderful bygone time when all we do is ask ourselves questions. I looked at all the prisoners and murmured under my breath, 'May the Lord be your holy keeper! Your lives are fragile. You are defenseless against the world that is crushing you, trampling you, casting you off like broken objects; and you're not even aware of it.' I lived with that weight upon my soul constantly."

As he said those words, my companion sighed heavily; not knowing how to answer his remarks, I felt ill at ease. It was obvious that the words were those of a man who was half-mad, but they stirred dark regions within me, awakening distant and painful echoes.

I was pondering these thoughts when he continued, in a somewhat spiteful tone.

"Those are men who have been discarded; they'll always live on the margins and be counted out. And why is that? Because they stole a loaf of bread one day, or a handful of rice. The worst part is that they don't even think about their condition. That's what disturbs me. And countless lives can be broken in that way! Just think about it! What taboo will keep you from doing harm? What taboo will preserve you from the harm someone might want to cause you? There are no taboos anywhere, there is nothing . . . The main thing isn't what's within you, or in the evil thought 'I'm going to steal,' but what is in the world that has made a yapping jackal out of you. For it isn't you who are rotten, it's the world. It's like an abscess that cannot come to a head."

Eyes half-closed, as if he were pursuing an elusive idea, the man whispered in a lifeless tone, "I realized that what had happened to me was unfair."

Then, unexpectedly, he smiled. An incredible freshness spread over his face.

"Yes," he said, "I'm thinking of my lawyer. He was a modern young man: hair slicked back, so stylish, knowledgeable, and what eloquence . . . ! He too was a friend of the underdog. But who are we in those people's eyes? He kept shouting, 'Who can say anything against this man?' None of the witnesses said a word . . .

"That is how he defended me. In fact, he defended me well. My murder only cost me a light sentence: five years in prison. Except, what happened after that? Everything went back to normal; nothing changed."

My interlocutor stopped talking, lifted his glass and swallowed a gulp of tea. Then he cleared his throat and went on calmly.

"That's why I say lawyers are a bunch of jokers; defend me when I still need to be defended, defend me before my crime, and don't allow me to reach that point . . . Afterward it's too late . . . ! Once I get started, no one can set me straight, I'll carry through to the end, I'll run until I fall. You can tie me up, but it's the world that needs to be changed, fools! And above all, don't try to teach me how to live; the man standing before you just might be able to give you a few lessons about that. No, give me the means with which to live! Why don't you understand that? Condemn me severely, condemn me to death; that might be best . . . It's your world that disgusts me. It is the source of too much human suffering. It would be better just to do away with us. If not . . . if not . . . our arms will grow and get longer and longer. When we've had enough of the dregs, we will be the ones to do away with you."

Having said those words, he fell silent again. He remained motionless. Even his features froze. That stillness along with the silence gradually gave rise—I could sense it—to fear: I was afraid of the man facing me. I cast about for something to say to him, but could find nothing.

He was the one who began talking again.

"Bitch of a life . . . ," he cursed clearly.

But it wasn't a complaint, there was much too much indifference in those words. He was evidently thinking of something else.

Nevertheless, I thought to myself, "Now here's a man who has thought things over! He's arrived at a conclusion that I cannot refute without contradicting myself."

I remained silent. As if he hadn't noticed, he declared again loudly, "Bitch of a life . . ."

That time I detected a touch of gentleness in his dreamy voice. There was still not the echo of a complaint in his words. The stranger had obviously reached a state of serene lucidity.

That degree of lucidity was unspeakably distressing to me, and I knew that if I remained silent I would go mad—just as he was!

15

AT THE CAFÉ

Just then, he asked me if he might order some more tea. We were on our second teapot; he insisted.

"Why not? I have the money, I earned it in prison."

He patted the pocket of his suit jacket with the palm of his hand, making the coins jingle.

"You're in no hurry," he said. "You have nothing to do at this time of the night. So stay."

That evening, I stayed even longer than usual at the café. Outside in the street, dark raindrops as thick as pitch splashed and gurgled unremittingly.

FORBIDDEN LANDS

The women shielded their eyes with both hands. The light slashed through the atmosphere which, though the sun remained hidden, was filled with a vivid glare.

Intrigued, they observed the silhouette of the man who had appeared at the bottom of the incline. From up here the land falls in a steep slope, and then dips imperceptibly. That large June bug was climbing up, waving its antennae in the empty grayness.

A few red and ochre mud houses were set down on the bare rock jutting out here and there on top of the hill. All around, the land bristled with dried stems clicking in the wind. The stubble sticking up from the ground was reddening as far as the eye could see. Up on this remote hilltop, the tousled and stubborn olive trees cast elusive shadows.

The visitor virtually sprang up, enormous, though bent with age, at the very top of the hill. His body was wrapped in a grimy and tattered robe. Untidy, covered with powdery earth, he seemed exhausted, unspeakably weary. "As if," thought the women watching him, "he'd come from far away, from very far away."

In the passageway, hardly paying attention to his arrival, children were chasing round in excited circles. Suddenly they were shrieking, buoyed by an explosion of joy. Dirty rags hung in shreds around their legs; the tumultuous gang leaped tirelessly this way and that, absorbed in their game.

Scattered around on several sides, infants—some with bare bottoms, others with handfuls of flies sucking at their pus-filled eyes—crawled about in the dust.

Women stood in front of each house, a flap of their tunics

pulled up over their heads. They stared at the stranger. Called to him from a distance.

"What have you come up here for, good man?" asked one of them.

Panting, the man began to bellow gruffly.

"One of your men is named Tahar. He lives in this hamlet, this *dechra!* . . . He's the one I want to see . . ."

His voice gurgled and then strangled at the back of his throat. Two women went out to meet him; reaching him, one of them took his stick, put the old man's deeply creased hand on her shoulder, while the other held him up by the arm.

Together, the three of them walked up to the houses.

"There, rest now."

"Thank you, my dears," uttered the stranger in a wheezing voice.

The other women gradually approached, examined the intruder with calm looks. From time to time they chided the yellow dogs sniffing at the ground around their feet.

The youngsters continued leaping about in the background and letting out shrill cries.

"So it's Tahar you're looking for. What do you want of him?" asked the peasant woman who had first called out to him.

The stranger nodded his head, trying to catch his breath.

Still heaving, he managed to say, "Send for him. I have to talk to him . . ."

Turning toward the mountains, the woman began a long, modulated call.

"Yaaa, Ta-haar!" She repeated this two or three times.

The echo rolled the name she had called around in the air.

The answer came back deep and full.

"Yaaa!"

"Come down . . . Someone needs to see you . . ."

It took the fellahs quite some time to arrive; they came out in front of the houses.

"Hey, *viejo,* welcome to you," said one of them. "What brings you to our dechra?"

The stranger didn't answer, but was panting noisily. Sweat trickled slowly along the deep wrinkles lining his forehead, cheekbones, temples, before running into the gray beard, coarse as tow. His face was taking on metallic reflections, which his black skin made all the shinier.

The men made a circle around him after having pushed the women back. Sitting on the ground, leaning to one side, the old man was grasping his stick; a few of the men squatted down on their heels near him. The others stood waiting.

"Breathe easily, good man. We're in no hurry," said one of the mountain men.

The man who had spoken made signs to a woman who was walking away.

"Today you'll stay in the douar, if you want to, eh? You'll spend the night there."

The vagabond shook his head.

"By God!" replied the fellah, "there's no need to go any farther."

Everyone agreed.

Just then the woman who had left the group returned: she carried a jug in one hand and in the other, half a loaf of flat bread.

"Have a nice cool drink of water," said the peasant woman.

She set down the enamelware jug before the guest and laid the flat bread on top of it. Then she stepped away.

"I cannot stay," said the man. "But I've brought this."

He rummaged through his clothing; from his rags he extricated a bundle of printed papers.

"Which one of you is Tahar?"

He stared fixedly at the fellahs.

"Me. What is it?"

"I was to give them to you, Tahar. So here they are. I think you know what they are for."

The man named Tahar was making ready to get to his feet, papers in hand.

"Wait. Listen to me, everyone listen; *they've* beaten one of your people. Sadak is his name," added the old man.

They remained silent. A few women moaned.

"That's enough," scolded one of the fellahs. "Go back to your homes!"

"Go and get him," said the old man.

"Where is he?" the men asked.

Tahar walked over toward Bachir's shop. At the same time, the other men left in the direction the stranger had indicated.

"I'll catch up with you," said Tahar.

There were only women left in the company of the outsider.

"Why did they hurt him?" one of them wailed. "Oh, poor man!"

"What did he do to them?" the eldest wanted to know.

"Nothing. But you know how it is."

"Ya ha!" shouted the peasant women.

"He was talking about voting," groaned the vagabond.

"Did he have anything to gain from it?"

"He wanted to explain to our people . . . It was in everyone's interest. We would be able to choose the men who would speak on our behalf before the nation. But not everyone *up there* wants to hear the voice of the people. So this is what happens!"

"It needed to be explained," said the old woman.

She asked the women around her, "Isn't that right, all of you? Isn't that right, Zahra bent Mhammed?"

"Yes, Lalla Fatma."

"Isn't that right, Halima, Kheyra, Alia?"

"Yes," said the women.

"Isn't that right, Salma?"

Salma, who had grown heavy and languid because of her pregnancy, had also wanted to come see the visitor. Even Salma acquiesced. The faces of these peasant women were kneaded out of firm clay in which their gaze lit up a transparent gleam. A worried flame flickered in their eyes.

"There are many who explain," the man agreed. "But it's not easy for our people to make their voices heard." The old man laughed in short bursts. "You don't really believe that the law could be on our side, do you?" He contemplated his wrinkled hand and seemed to be thinking. He squinted his eyes.

"And there are millions of us," he said dreamily.

He fidgeted about, attempted to rise to his feet, but had to ask for the help of one of the peasant women, who pulled him up by the hands.

A few moments later, his silhouette was growing smaller on the slope.

"He drank the water," Salma remarked. "The flat bread hasn't been touched."

"That man might not have a family or any relatives," Fatma said with a quaver in her voice. "That is a very sad situation for a human being."

And without anyone understanding why, she mumbled, "Every single one of us could be in need of help."

Then, as if to herself, she said, "Hey, we're all poor, and it's the same everywhere."

"He goes from douar to douar," Salma said again. "And makes friends."

"We'll need a lot of kindness to face the misfortune. If not, we'll start to resemble wild beasts."

Sadak had been brought to Bachir's house; he lay stretched out as if he weren't suffering at all, but his life was escaping from his wounds.

"You might tell me I'm going to die. But we are strong," he murmured.

He seemed to be addressing invisible beings.

"Our people are good."

And his body shuddered. His face darkened with a hot flush. He was panting; it was horrible. From then on, his breath came only in short gasps.

A long time, a very long time afterward, he said, "It will be in combat that they will be able to show their true nature."

His voice had grown calm again, serene.

He was too young, he claimed, to fear death. In the peace of his heart, in spite of all the horrors, he'd found renewed faith that a life of hope was possible. He had been carrying that faith within him for a long time.

"When you're well . . . ," Ali began.

Relentlessly, swarms of flies were buzzing, whirling overhead, swooping down upon Sadak. Sitting by his side, Tahar tirelessly waved a long branch back and forth.

Sadak cut in on Ali abruptly.

"I can't . . ."

After that, his reply broke off, then resumed.

"I'm not afraid of death . . ."

It was as if the words had been formulated outside his body and then drifted off into the distance.

"They thought this was fine land? They've robbed us of it? But mankind is awakening. It's opening its eyes. They only know how to offend it, to harm it. And they don't even have the instinct for death! When it comes time to die, they will lack the will to do so. They are fooling themselves. Ha! Ha! They think they want to try strong-arming us, but their sole reward will be the darkness of the grave."

And he remained silent for a moment.

Tahar asked Ali in a low voice, "Have all our friends been informed?"

"Is that Baba Salem speaking?" asked Sadak.

"No, Tahar," said the other.

Sadak extended his arm and touched his hand. Tahar turned his face away and tears sprang from his eyes.

Holding their arms close to their bodies, they were waiting to be able to go in. The shop, a large, low room, was part of the house: a corridor dug into the hillside led to it. The very narrow door only allowed one man to be admitted at a time. All around that dark mouth, the wall, baked hard like a piece of pottery, was painted white. Some of them left their babouches at the doorstep.

Inside, people were seated on the tamped earth floor. Still others were leaning up against the walls with their hands behind their backs. Five or six fellahs were squeezed up on the only bench to be found there. A rush of murmurs flowed out of the shop.

The only light filtered in, pulsating, from the door. On a counter and some shelves, which faded into the half-light, were cakes of soap, a stack of espadrilles, some sugarloaves. Set down on the floor, yawning sacks filled with barley, corn, chickpeas. At the back of the room, a piece of sackcloth was hung over a passageway pierced in the wall. When one came to fetch something, he'd call out and see Bachir come through that hole.

Ba Hamida, the village elder, came in. He saw all the people there; his mouth started working behind a sparse, ashen beard. But no sound came out. It was a habit of his; he kept chewing away without saying anything.

People moved aside for Ba Hamida, who took a seat next to Tahar.

Each newcomer greeted everyone and cast a look around the room. Soon it became difficult to find a place to sit.

Tahar began to speak slowly. The conversations that had struck up ceased. At first he spoke in such a low voice he could hardly be heard. Close-set blue eyes lit his face with an intense expression. Over his worn clothing he wore faded cowherd's overalls.

"You all know why we are holding this meeting today. It's about the elections . . . And you all know how elections go in our country. This time, *they* have beaten Sadak. They nearly struck him dead. You all know that . . . Will he live, will he die? No one can say what will happen. But they've done a good job on him, men. And why? Because we were told: you are free to vote . . . Sadak was explaining that to our brothers. 'Now that we've got our candidate,' he was saying, 'the fellahs need to be told about it.' He worked day and night, never resting. I want everyone to understand that. Was he right or wrong? Whatever the case may be, at first he began to have problems with the community police officer. Then there was trouble with the local governor. Sadak was like a lion, he always knew how to stand up for himself. He'll always be like a lion . . . Ever since that day, he was a marked man. He had to battle with the authorities every day. And this morning, the gendarmes came. Have you seen the condition they left him in?"

He stared sharply at the audience. In his hand he was swinging a stick with a crook for a handle.

With a slight quaver in his voice, he began again, "If I'm talking to you about Sadak, it's to show you how elections are run here. This is how they are run. This is how free we are to vote. What happened to Sadak is happening to all of our people! Should we bow our necks under the yoke? Are we willing to accept the will of the administrator or stay away from the voting booths? It's easy to give in. But what about shame? How can one deal with shame? It is indispensable for a man to remain standing firmly on both legs."

Tahar punctuated his speech, making light taps with his cane on the floor.

The fellahs weren't working, there was nothing left to do in the fields. At this time of year, they'd already done the seeding. Some of them lived on bits of land that the bare rock tore to shreds. So they'd done the seeding. Barley, durum wheat. Whatever they were able to.

In summer, their harvest would fill but a few sacks; they would store it underground, in silos: that's what gave their bread such a good, strong taste;—and they would use their grain parsimoniously.

But they hadn't counted on the drought. In truth, they'd been caught off guard: in their situation, anyone else would have been too, no matter the extent of their knowledge and pretensions.

Then they had remarked, "It'll be another fine day! . . ." and in the dazzling shower of sunlight, the colors of life paled. The wind swept round the circus of hills, stabbed through the mass of bluing mountains, gusted about every tree, shook its winnowing baskets onto the fields opened out toward the arid sky.

The ground remained gray, yellow . . . The plowed earth offered itself up avidly. But nothing came to deliver it. Nothing other than that beating of wings scraping against the air and snapping like a sagging sail.

The wind, the sunlight, sucked at the dark and vital core. The seed perished. The hope of harvest was buried up in those hills.

The people went out to contemplate their fields, lifted their eyes to the sky, then walked back, keeping to themselves. They wandered about here, there. Their vague gaze swept over the land. The tip of a burning ember glowed deep in their eyes.

These men are hard and austere. They are not accustomed to divertissements and have no distractions. Their violent tangles with the land take the place of everything else in life: the past, the future, happiness, grief . . . Everything you might learn, everything a man might feel during his lifetime.

To come here and talk to them about elections at a time like this! Worrying them sick with these questions! With these items and preambles. Gendarmes who massacre people, and all sorts of stories. The local governor, the community policeman, and their kind: they can all be damned! Who was in a better position to appreciate that? Ah, if only they were better informed about it all! All they really wanted was simply not even to hear about it at all. And speaking of shame . . . Shame . . . and other items and preambles . . . No one enjoys bowing their neck under the yoke, that's for sure. A man wants to hold his head up high. But does that mean we have no choice but to go out and allow ourselves to be beaten to death? Let's all go and get massacred. Life in this world would leave us in peace at last! If that's not what you want, what is? Since they gave us this freedom to vote and then regretted it, let them take it back. A lot of good it will do them. It won't make our barley grow.

"If only the polling station was in the nearby center as it used to be," Tahar was saying now. "But it has been transferred thirty miles away from here. When we get there the henchmen who recognize us won't let us in. Or else the polling station itself will be closed. Or better yet, there will only be ballots for the administrative candidate. Threatening us with aimed carbines, they'll force us to use them. The ballot box will probably be stuffed at the last minute anyway. We have to fight, men, fight . . . What do you expect? If we want to rise from the shadows . . . We are a force, a great force. If not, why so much cheating? Why do the authorities strike out? Why?"

And the fellahs pursued their thoughts: Why are there punitive expeditions? Why do the police patrol the countryside? Why were the houses of everyone who was neither a hatchet man nor an informer searched? Yes, why? Even the Foreign Legion has had a tour of duty here . . .

Just then, from the back of the shop, a woman's voice could be heard coming from the small opening. It came from inside the house.

"Sadak doesn't recognize anyone anymore."

Some men shook their heads without uttering a word.

"He won't make it through the night," whispered Ali.

As the seconds went by one by one, the fellahs thought of nothing else but that death.

Tahar looked at everyone, swallowed his saliva. His brow furrowed; he came up against something hard, like a knot, inside himself. But after the initial shock, tensing his muscles, he went on.

"We, the men of these mountains, declare that the whole country should rise up and spit with contempt in the face of the oppressor!"

The nascent furrow continued in a straight line.

"Should the outrages, the torture, and everything they put our people through change nothing? Should we let them go on, as long as we don't have to deal directly with them?"

Tahar walked heavily over to stand among the others. Whenever something needed to be said—something particularly important—this mountain man, in the prime of life, spoke to them all. If he ventured to take the floor, he struck hard and deep, just as he did when holding a pick. He knew there was nothing more to add.

Ali stood up.

"You probably don't all agree with what Tahar just said. Deep down inside, you may think otherwise. And perhaps one can think otherwise . . . Though I don't believe any other way of thinking is possible. Can we claim that these questions don't concern us? Our blood is being let. We must think it over. But you've heard all this before . . ."

An irritated voice shouted, "Just tell us what you want us to do, for God's sake!"

It was Ba Hamida who had cut in that way.

"Tahar gave us the explanation," he protested further, "that's enough. It was time to stop talking: he stopped talking. Now what must be done?"

Tahar lifted his head, stared hard at the audience. A bright light shone in his eyes; that light spilled over onto the men gathered there.

From where he was standing beside his friends he said, "Do you see those printed papers over there on the counter? They are our voting ballots. They must be distributed tonight to our neighbors in the region."

Silence spread over the crowd, and he added, "Even if you don't all agree, you won't refuse to help us."

In the dark night that nestled in the fields, the sound of stones rolling echoed out.

"So you really don't want one of us to come with you, Ba Hamida?"

"No! I don't need anyone," said the old man.

"It's dangerous, these days, all alone . . ."

Ba Hamida's halting laughter ricocheted through the night.

The others remained silent. Their shapes melted into the darkness.

The old man spoke again.

"I know paths they would never find, even in the middle of the day."

"Yes, of course."

"Each time night falls," Ba Hamida went on, "this country becomes ours again . . . It reverts to us."

"We've got to make it just as much ours in the daytime as well," commented a voice.

The men couldn't see each other, but each of them felt the warmth of the others nearby.

"Through fighting," someone said.

"May peace be with you. Adieu!"

Ba Hamida was already walking away.

"The people above us behave like criminals," a fellah declared.

As if he hadn't said enough he added, "They are tearing us apart, destroying us."

From the darkness came the answer, "Why? Because the people are lifting their heads. And so they tremble and strike out in rage."

They all recognized Tahar's voice.

"But they're wasting their strength," the other said. "No matter what they do, they'll lose in the end. They only know how to wreak havoc on the world, not how to heal it. Everything they do has an evil purpose. No force will be found to transform that evil into good . . . The evil will devour them, rot them away . . ."

"And we will bury them," said Tahar's voice afterward.

In pairs, they went out to crisscross the region, making no more noise than the earth respiring. They went out to wake up the peasants all over the countryside. The people had closed themselves up in their shacks; the messengers knocked at their doors. In a flash, the wavering flame of a torch lit up the faces of the fellahs. They had already been recognized by the sounds of their voices. From the opaque darkness, only the faces stood out, gently caressed by the touch of the light. The visitors handed over the papers and plunged back into the shadows.

The two brothers were going back to the village. Each footpath, each stone along the way, was familiar to them; they would have known the way with their eyes closed. They had been walking a long time, tirelessly, as if night eradicated all distances.

Along the way, they had only exchanged a few brief words, each of them—absorbed in his own thoughts—was listening to the calm voices that dwelt within. Around them, the restless night, the rushing clamor of the wind over the peaks . . . The same endless and accursed prophesies of death, terror, spilled blood drifted up to haunt them. At times, the recollection of Sadak's death, like a dark gust, swept over their hearts. Yet, the younger of the two, Laarej, could sense a hint of latent harmony filled with enthusiasm, with new spring sap, and hidden gentleness. Before he'd left the hamlet, his wife, Salma, had begun feeling pains.

When they reached the remote and solitary peaks they had started out from, Laarej saw a ray of light shining in the distance.

"In my opinion, this night will not come to an end without bringing new tidings," he predicted to Tahar. "Look, people are up at my house. All the women are there, and certainly yours is as well."

Laarej spoke in a calm and confident tone of voice; Tahar followed after him.

They could both now make out the excitement inside the shack. They pushed open the door.

The gentle flickering of a candle flame shone in the shadow-filled room. Near that source of warm red light arose the sound of a prayer being recited. Doudja, the bonesetter, was there, Doudja who assisted in deliveries and deaths with equal expertise. The air was heavy with the magical smells of incense and *adad,* elder root, which is burned for its fragrance at the time of delivery.

Covered with pieces of cloth that concealed them entirely, save their faces, the women were gathered on one side of the shack, their shapes barely distinguishable in the cocoon of soft folds. Their faces seemed to be sculpted by the light, which brightly hemmed the edges of the cloths over their heads. Tahar and Laarej squatted down in an out-of-the-way place, like the women waiting quietly in the shadows.

Doudja, the old bonesetter, was chanting her litanies incessantly. In that way and in a thousand others, each inflection that came from her throat was aimed at conjuring evil spells. Accompanying her and backing her up like a shadow follows the body, the winds were faintly sounding a cold harsh refrain over the desolate heights.

Doudja's full-throated droning ceased. Then other monotone voices rose up, drawing out: those of the women sitting before Salma who, of like age and experience, shared the same standing. With identical intonations and harshness, their voices came together in unison.

29

FORBIDDEN LANDS

A scream rang out suddenly and it was like a plummeting projectile streaking through the night.

The pains pressing Salma were not going to let up; when her wild plaints rang out again, the matrons fell silent. The restless night itself seemed to be waiting; it had grown calmer, was making sweet sighs to itself, deep rumblings that rolled all the way out to the horizon.

Other screams followed, screams that broke, and then were reborn. And then something happened in a flash. The young woman, raised up by the older ones, grabbed hold of a pole that ran the width of the shack; the women tied her wrists together. With her body hanging in the air, and laboring with the pain, Salma filled the night with her tremendous clamor. The women went back to their flat and lugubrious litanies. Salma twisted even harder; her screams drew out horrifically and then sank into a lament.

Once more, the litanies ceased. Suddenly the plaint rose again in another surge, rose still higher, and swept through their hearts like a dense, infinite fog, then dissipated into a hoarse, grim, unbroken groaning.

Old Doudja pushed the men outside. They had barely passed through the door when all sound stopped. The shack remained mute. Several minutes passed . . .

All at once, a stubborn wailing broke forth. The two men went in. While the women began their chants again, the newborn child, who had been received in some rags, was anointed with olive oil over his entire body. The mother was lying on a mat, eyes closed. On her face was an expression that set her apart from ordinary human beings; it was as if she were on the very brink of life.

The neighbor women had brought sugar and coffee tied up tightly in handkerchiefs for this eventuality. As soon as the baby boy had been swaddled, his gender identified and announced with cries of "You, You!" called out to the four cardinal points—just one woman took on the task of doing so, and repeated it only three times, because the fellahs were in mourning—the fire was stirred, dried twigs set ablaze, and hot coffee prepared for everyone. The sun rose; it was as if, at that very instant, a faceless, shapeless guest had walked into the shack like an old friend. The flame of the candle waned. The peasants fell into a vague, all-pervasive sense of waiting, like the soft glow straying out over the highlands.

Doudja, with her oracular voice, proffered, "A Sadak has left us, a Sadak has been born."

With her voice hardly audible, she recited a prayer in a rapid, fervent whisper.

"May he be preserved from all pitfalls! May life be as a light to him! May happiness be upon him!"

Another dark, glad chant flowed timidly out of the shack. It rolled around in the mountains in the cold raw dawn for a long time, tumbled down the muddy paths to meet the wind that whipped the frozen wasteland of the plateaus.

LITTLE COUSIN

She descended the sole step of the porch; at first it was that sunlight which struck her as odd. She stopped in her tracks. In the same instant, she felt like turning around and going back. But she was already almost in the middle of the street. The reverberations stung her eyes. Tears brimmed at her lids. All the way out to the very end, the row of houses in front of her was dissolving in the sunlight. It was only the presence of certain details, a door, a balcony—both black—that gave the street any semblance of reality. Mansouria, Little Cousin, went back under the porch roof, took three or four steps . . . stopped again. Only one sound broke the numbed noonday silence, that of her worn babouches scuffing over the large polished slabs of gray stone. The place was filled with dusk light. She could barely make out the two palm trees nodding over their metal drums on either side. She could barely even be sure they were still standing there, in the same place. The persistent image of the sizzling street filled her vision, the compact light, of a gray hue, played tricks with her mind. It made her forget her sorrow. A truck turned into the street and the walls quaked. The roar of its motor echoed through the emptiness. Periodically, the pain would disappear, then come surging back. It ended up settling into a dull aching spot in her chest. The sound of the truck fading into the distance was no more than a faint quivering. Little Cousin tried to moan as if she were still in the hospital; she was suffering now, that was it, she was suffering. She no longer felt that horrid apathetic despair. "I don't want to! I don't want to!" was all she could manage to groan. She really would have to leave. But she didn't want to go back to the stables, back to the *cuadra*.

Suddenly the suffering left her. The rumbling of the truck ceased. She had to go back to the cuadra now.

The door that led into the hospital was dark green. Little Cousin couldn't resist and pushed on the door, which swung open before her. She found herself in a covered walkway, bordering a large courtyard laid with red tiles. She couldn't understand why they had decided to throw her out of this place. She recalled that same cleanliness everywhere, that cleanliness which had become familiar to her. The new, colonial-style edifice was already beginning to show signs of disrepair. Something about it was reminiscent of a public building. A feeling of satisfaction crept back into Mansouria's heart. To be forced to leave . . . She'd been telling herself for the last few minutes that she wouldn't be able to; now she was making her way along the walkway lined with pillars, she ran her hand gently over the smooth cold gray wash on the walls. She felt vaguely content.

She continued along the walkway, which was bathed in coolness. She would be so grateful if she could enter *his* service, if there were chores for her to do: sweep and wash the floors, wipe the windows . . . She was busy with those thoughts when she saw a little door at the end of the walkway. Closed. One couldn't say what detail about that door made it seem to lead to an underground passageway; it did not breach the wall as do most doors. Instead, it had been made like a sort of incision. The entire top part of the door, a meter from the floor, was made of small opaque panes of glass. Little Cousin was lost in thought. In the last seven days she'd come to know this building well, she'd come to know it by heart. The wall to her left had scratches on it, it looked as if it had been marked by fingernails; higher up ogled the eye of a narrow casement window; up ahead, the wards . . . The door opened. A man, his hand on the doorknob and his face turned toward the inside, was holding it half-open. His voice and someone else's deep inside the room nevertheless reached the ears of Little Cousin, who could hear everything—the sound of the conversation, the cheerful tone of the two men—but who did not understand a word of what they were saying. They were Frenchmen. It was the Head Doctor and another Frenchman.

Just then, the man pushed the door all the way open and went out, followed by the Doctor, who, still young, clean shaven, had a pleasantly fresh face. He walked past without seeing her. But suddenly stopped, after having taken several steps, and turned around.

"Are you still here?" he asked. "Go on, now. Don't hang around here."

Mansouria understood. The Head Doctor was motioning with his hand; she understood she had to leave. The Head Doctor was not a cruel man, Little Cousin knew that. She had even sensed a note of kindness in his voice.

And he left her there. Went off to join the other Frenchman. The Head Doctor had finished his work there: he only came to the indigenous hospital for a few hours in the morning.

Little Cousin was still holding a small square of folded paper in the palm of her hand. Now she began to shake. Suddenly she was seized with panic again. There was no one left for her to see. She held her breath. She was overcome with a violent fit of trembling that sent dark waves washing through her soul.

The Head Doctor had called for her that morning, and the Moorish woman who looked after the patients had come with her. Wearing her white apron, the woman looked a little like a European.

"Fatma, tell her . . . ," the Head Doctor had ordered.

As he spoke, Fatma translated for Little Cousin: "All right now, we can't keep you in the hospital anymore," said the Head Doctor. "It's not easy . . . We've got too many patients, we don't know where to put them. And also, in your case, it's that we don't have a ward for contagious diseases . . . Pulmonary tuberculosis . . . Take this paper, the Head Doctor has noted on it that you were treated here for seven days."

Little Cousin could not figure out what had gone on in the Head Doctor's mind. But why, why had he always been so kind? And why today? She'd done nothing he could blame her for. Did he have one little unfair thing to blame on her? She hadn't offended him once since she'd been there. So why?

"The Head Doctor also says . . . it's no use coming back. Patients who have been released from here can't be treated again. We don't want to hear anything more about them."

She recalled the first day when the Head Doctor had come in person to ask what she would like to eat. She had been allowed a liter of milk. A liter, bless my soul. She had been filled with a sort of glow. She had a whole liter all for herself. Little Cousin hadn't had a taste of milk since she had stopped suckling her mother. And there she was an old woman. And she had a liter of milk all to herself.

"Will there at least be some left for the others?" she had asked herself worriedly that day, observing the other patients in the ward.

"You need to eat well," the Head Doctor had said. "Fruit, meat . . ."

Uncontrollably, tears sprang from her eyes. Little Cousin wept, ashamed at herself for having given rise to such kindness.

Then they had changed her clothing and put her in a bed, she who had never lain between a pair of sheets. Who had never even heard of a bed!

Mansouria went out into the sun-bleached street. Bare feet stuck into her babouches, she could feel the heat rising up from the pavement around her legs like burning ashes. The blazing August noon light reverberated mercilessly off the walls. The town was sunk in torpor. From time to time she was shaken with sudden shivering. It seemed as if not a living soul lived in those houses. The cicadas alone reigned over the sweltering silence from up in the crowns of the trees around the hospital. All the vigor of the daylight was reduced to their strident extreme, to the loneliness surrounding Little Cousin.

Now she was beginning to get used to the anxiety which filled her, which was turning into a sort of forgetfulness, but which, even so, continued to hold her attention. She was able to reflect upon all the little nothings that made up her existence. And then she had the feeling that a world was closing up before her, a world she had only penetrated by accident, like one might open the wrong door, a forbidden world. She would go back to her cuadra.

In the cuadra, men, women, chickens, donkeys, children, romped around together between the shacks, jabbering, pecking, nibbling, wallowing, bawling. The kids went around black and grimy with tangled, matted mops. They ran after one another and wrestled furiously in the rubble. In the center of the cuadra, an immense pile of refuse, manure, and debris, higher than the others, formed a mound upon which weeds grew. Sitting in a circle all around it, shacks leaned up against the surrounding wall. All sorts of scrap metal were piled up in the corners; a fetid smell arose from the rotting metal. A gaggle of haggard, rambunctious children rejoiced around a broken-edged well that stood at the back of the courtyard.

Little Cousin would undoubtedly be welcomed by the piercing cries of Eduardo's wife, the gypsy woman and her daughter Pamela, if at that time the two women weren't away in the Arab neighborhoods selling multicolored ribbons, tulle, and lace to the Moorish housewives, crying out in front of every door, *Aïe roflès! Aïe roflès!*

All day long, the steady pounding of the cooper's wooden mallet rose from Salah Esseban's workshop. There was always a fire lit between the staves of a barrel he was going to hoop. The flames licked the wood but never ate into it. Apprentices leaned over the rounded flanks of casks, wielding adzes.

Seeing her come into the cuadra, Salah Esseban would surely call out, "So, Little Cousin, you've come back? I swear to God, I'm happy to see you! I told you they'd take good care of you over there!"

It was Salah Esseban, the cooper, who had given her that crate of planks in which she would take shelter.

All of a sudden, Little Cousin began to think about death, her death. She thought, "I have to go to Dar Sbitar, to see Aïni and her children two or three times in the time that is left to me. I'll say, 'Aïni, Little Cousin,' and to the children, 'I'm very fond of you all, my children. May God forgive me, it's been so long since I've come to see you.' Two or three times, that's all. Poor Aïni, with her little ones, life's not easy. And I'll go to cousin Hasna's too. Just once, that's all. She and her husband are rich. I couldn't go see them more than once. Then I'll come back to my place and wait to die. It's not that I'm fed up with living. I'll surely miss all the kind people in this world. But I'll say to my death, 'Come to me, or I will come to you.' Of course I'll miss Aïni and her children . . . I'm old and tired. It's not old age that kills you. It's not death that kills you either. It's the life one inherits. Surely some charitable souls can be found to sew up my funeral shroud and give me a decent burial. *Ahbab Rabbi besef* (God's friends are numerous) . . . Our fellow beings are so numerous and fraternal. Is there anything more beautiful than life?"

A FINE WEDDING

Three women went calling from house to house, a town crier made the rounds of the city announcing the marriage celebration.

Therefore the three children, Aouicha, Omar, Mériem, were to spend the night at Aunt Hasna's; at first the boy refused to believe it. There had been so much talk about that marriage! To Omar, it was one of those events that people keep trumpeting about but that can never really happen. The plans were just too wonderful, too grandiose.

On top of it all, Aouicha had just come back from there and was enumerating to them all the dishes being prepared. Aïni and the little ones were listening to her, not being able to believe their ears. Aouicha started swearing; they knew well enough that all those things were served at rich people's weddings!

But that they should actually be among the invited, that was what was difficult for them to imagine. Suddenly the nuptials took on incredible grandeur.

The four of them just stood there in silence for a moment. Even Aouicha seemed dazed.

"But that's not the end of the matter," said Aïni suddenly.

She too had sunk into the dream for a few seconds; abruptly, she brushed away those bright filaments.

"That's not the end of the matter, children. Listen closely to what your mother is going to say. Taste the dishes that people offer you *over there* but barely touch them at all."

"Boo, Ma!" groaned Aouicha.

"Did you hear me? Barely touch them. I'll be keeping my eye on you."

The children seemed devastated. They stood there examining her.

Changing her tone, Aïni said in a whisper, "I don't want it said that my children are dying of hunger . . . That we're only going to the marriage to eat. However poor one is, one must hold on to his pride."

"For people like us," thought Omar, "living means eating. And the joy of living, the joy of eating."

His mother's words were buzzing in his mind.

"A bit of pride is quite essential in a life like ours," she was saying. "Whether one is a cobbler or a weaver, one must hold his head high and walk up to people as if he were a Rothschild."

For large commemorative ceremonies, marriages, circumcisions, any major occasion, the presence of children is an absolute must, without them nothing would matter. In our town, it's impossible to imagine anything happening without children playing a primary role. At the entrance to the neighborhood a detachment of youngsters, girls and boys, were obstructing the narrow street. It was they who lent that joyous atmosphere to Aunt Hasna's house. The few children who were garbed in party clothes stood out as oddly as trees turned green in winter. The others resembled Omar and were wearing nondescript outfits. They were running excitedly around after one another, yelping at the top of their lungs. The smaller ones were crying.

It truly was the extraordinary event everyone had been expecting, had been hoping it would be. An all-pervasive heady euphoria, a jubilant atmosphere reigned there.

Meantime the women were already coming in and gathering inside the house. A woman is always quite drawn to a wedding announcement. It's almost always the same story. One of them gets invited to a wedding celebration somewhere? She begs her husband to allow her to go. The head of the family immediately takes refuge in frowning silence. Finally he gives in. In truth he could hardly refuse her something of that nature. Happier than ever, the woman then dons all her finery.

It also happens—and frequently too—that more people show up than have been invited.

A FINE WEDDING

The first women to arrive filed into a room into which new guests poured endlessly. Newcomers lined up against the walls each in turn. All the women were staring avidly at the bride, who was seated on a chair in a hieratical pose. With her face entirely hidden by a gold brocade veil, she remained immobile.

It was not permissible for her to speak! But it was possible for her to move. Should that occur, she must quickly—and without drawing much attention—regain her imperturbable posture.

No matter what kind of character she has, a bride must not show it in any way on the wedding day. The bride on that day remained inaccessible; moreover to her, traditions were all too solemn, of such an awe-inspiring solemnity, she wouldn't have dared move so much as an eyelash. That is why the women guests were so deeply moved in spite of themselves.

At that moment, all the gravity hovering in the room was concentrated upon her; the guests were conversing in low voices, even if that is an impossible task for a woman. But soon, as the talk grew livelier, a discreet murmur rose from one end of the large room to the other. The women seemed to be steeped in pleasant ceremoniousness, in affable respect.

"Don't forget, dear," one of them was explaining, "that men today like wives who dress well and keep them company."

The response came promptly, "She has enough in her trousseau to clothe herself for ten years!"

The woman who had spoken first added haughtily, "Her trousseau? You'll see it in just a minute!"

Another woman, from the husband's side undoubtedly, declared nonchalantly, "Her trousseau must be just like all the others."

"No, my dear," said the first lady, flushed and agitated. "It is not like the others. Every man or woman who's seen it has been left gaping. Everyone knows what we spent on it . . ."

A very old relative implored, "Today is a blessed day . . . May this house be filled with harmony . . ."

Those words seemed to smooth over conflicts that would

have plenty of opportunities to erupt: the discussion died back down.

Thereupon, the children arrived. They slipped through, pinching the arms and calves of the women who were crowding together to keep them from passing and, having almost slithered along on their bellies, stood up in front of the bride. Her magnificence drew the eye irresistibly. Omar would have liked to fill his heart with that image. Draped in gold lamé, or silver brocade fabrics that fell all the way to her feet, she was sitting up straight on her chair; calm, not a quiver ran through her; only her breath lifted her chest. A pointed headdress embroidered with golden threads, studded with glittering spangles, rose above her forehead; hanging from the point of the headdress, the veil, which hid her features from view, fell down to her shoulders. Standing in front of that faceless idol, Omar felt strangely flustered.

Her visage was only uncovered for certain women. Even then a female relative in charge of the task had to agree to exhibiting her; the bride remained as still as if she were sunk in profound slumber. When the veil was lifted, her perfectly immobile face and closed eyelids appeared in a flash of shimmering jewelry and silk. Her forehead, lips, cheeks were spread with nothing but pearl, pink, and crimson. A small colored circle decorated each cheekbone. The whiteness of her arms, which could be observed at leisure, cast snowy reflections upon her clothing. Her hands, adorned with many rings, resting on her knees, showed a fine latticework of henna traced all the way up to her elbows. Her nails and the palms of her hands had been dyed. Such a demure, detached demeanor! One would have thought the bride was unaware of the pomp and splendor that was being displayed upon her, around her—and for her!

Suddenly there was a ripple of restless agitation.

Have the little rascals go outside!

The children had to make their way out again. Opening their ranks to let them pass, the women harassed them, some rewarding them with a slap, others a shove, until they had all been kicked out. Crying out louder than justified by the blows, the children fled in an indescribable tumult, proffering insults . . .

They went gallivanting across the courtyard. But other women were waiting for them there, who chased after them.

Then everyone played at running after one another in an atmosphere of general confusion. Meanwhile the women guests kept flocking in. The hubbub, the crowd, the multitude of dresses, colors waving this way and that, were becoming dizzying. One couldn't imagine what kind of wild rejoicing might break loose with a fury at any moment.

One little girl suggested, "Let's play getting married!"

The boys remained indifferent.

The girls repeated, "Come on, let's play getting married!"

They vied with one another, repeating, "Getting married! Getting married!"

And they made a circle round the boys, who—closed in on all sides—ended up giving in.

Omar pointed to his aunt's bedroom: he knew how to get in. Climbing the steps to the second floor, he motioned to the others, who followed him up one by one. He lifted the shutter hook of one of the windows: first he, then his companions, heaved themselves up and jumped into the room.

When everyone was there, they hid under Aunt Hasna's monumental bed. An incredibly high antique bed: in a sitting position, the children's heads didn't touch the underside. They sat in a circle; Yamina was chosen to be the bride. She accepted her role without saying a word. Her sweet oval face was solemn; she had long, smooth hair, green eyes. The groom was a lively, curly-headed boy. Silently, the little girl went and sat in front of him, waited. The children demanded that Yamina close her eyes. A piece of gauze taken from Aunt Hasna's wardrobe was draped over her. They all looked at one another. Then the groom, having made a decision, wet his finger with his saliva, and touched Yamina's abdomen.

Everyone in the house was jabbering and answering each other at once. The smells of stew and roasted meats wafted up from the ground floor. Sniffing those odors, the kids couldn't resist any longer and leapt back through the window.

In the courtyard, the group found that the small round low tables, known as *meïdas,* had been set up; the guests were serving themselves thick slices of lamb floating in a saffron sauce. Oh, all that meat!

Couscous laced with dates and quarters of hard-boiled eggs would be spooned over it. Aunt Hasna had really gone all out!

Certain women were eating with all five fingers. Their lipstick melted into the grease smearing their mouths. Meanwhile, sitting next to them, elegant women looked like jointed dolls.

The children wormed their way into all the groups, snatching here and there whatever they could, some leftover meat or bread. They went a little farther off to devour the remnants they'd swiped as quickly as they could. Pigeons flapped all around them, trying to get some crumbs.

Aunt Hasna, whose torso was bent forward from the small of her back, had her eye on everything; in a terrifying tone of voice, she was blaring out orders to the cooks, welcoming the women who were coming in. On her buxom hips shone a multicolored striped *foutah,* a piece of silk worn around the hips over a dress. An ample tunic with a small flower print draped her in a dignified manner. She didn't miss a single word being pronounced around her: she would reply; then burst out in throaty laughter, drink in the compliments—and laugh some more. Her eyes would then shrink to the point of becoming only narrow slits in her fleshy face and finally disappear all together. She was bursting with joy! She lorded over that population of women. Bright and straight, a flame burned within her that seemed to obliterate the contours of such a cumbersome body.

Omar sensed she had noticed him. At the exact same minute his aunt's pudgy hand grabbed his arm and quickly extirpated him from the swarm of kids whirling around everywhere.

"Go sit next to your mother," she whispered in his face. "She's over there."

She pointed Aïni out to him.

"Go on, before there's nothing left to eat!"

The boy rapidly wound his way through the guests pressing around the meïdas.

"There you are!" said Aïni.

She didn't look happy; she thought she should wear a severe expression in front of the other women.

"Sit down here."

She moved over a little, made room for him between herself and a stranger. The woman, head bowed, was swallowing mouthful after mouthful without stopping. She seemed detached from all the agitation around her; Omar stared at her. With a horrid sucking sound, she ingurgitated a slice of filet.

"One would think," exclaimed another woman at the table, "one would really think that some women haven't got a bite to eat at home! Boo!"

But the other woman didn't reply, for either she didn't think she was being alluded to or was pretending she hadn't heard the remark. Without saying a word, she continued to dig into the common dish with her thumb, her index, and her middle fingers. The woman who had made the remark had large features set in a handsome face marked with imposing and superior airs: she must surely have been the wife of a carpet maker or merchant. Aïni said nothing. Nevertheless she cast furtive glances at her poor neighbor. One could see the pity she felt; and, suddenly, her eyes filled with resentment.

Turning toward her son, she ordered, "Here, eat."

She broke her slice of bread, shoved a piece of it into his hands, then watched him with furrowed brows.

The boy reached his hand out toward the dish, and dipped his bread in unenthusiastically. After a moment, he stopped, a lump in his throat, not being able to go on eating.

Aïni also ate as if she were acting out of duty.

Not far from there, Aouicha and Mériem were chewing each mouthful with extreme difficulty.

"Are you full?" Aïni asked her son.

The woman with noble features broke in.

"That child hasn't eaten a thing!"

"Yes, of course, dear," Aïni said, dismissing her.

Then to Omar, she said, "Go play, son," in a gentle and inflexible voice.

The child contemplated the bread abandoned on the meïda with a kind of fascination, and walked away. He wouldn't have been able to say what thoughts were whirling through his mind. At first, with unbearable clarity, he felt pained astonishment. The feeling ran through him like a flame. Afterward, the question arose: "Why am I being denied bread?" And was soon followed by another: "Who is denying me bread?" His aunt would not miss that bread—white as milk, kneaded out of the finest flour—or those cakes either that the servants were beginning to pass around.

All the children in town, it seemed, had heard about the celebration. They came in gangs; wild, black from head to toe, they went up to the tables cautiously, sniffing. They were thrown a bone or a crust of bread and shooed off with a slap. They fled toward other groups.

Three of them stood still for a long time, their noses in the air, breathing in the smells. With feverish eyes, they stared at the guests who ate on and on, each gesture burning into their minds. When they were offered something, the strongest of the three grabbed it. The two others continued to watch the women wolfing down food.

An anxious clamor was growing louder each minute, consisting of calls, of orders yapped out in a shrill voice, shouts: a thousand conversations, the laments of the women roasting the meat who were swamped with work, and the barking of dogs that had been drawn by the profusion of smells mingling in the air. It only lasted an instant. The tide of starving children was pushed back to the gate, which was locked and which two negresses kept firmly closed. But in the meantime, the youngsters' raid had been devastating. In a flash the guests had seen pieces of meat disappear into thin air, greedy claws close over quarter and half loaves of bread, entire dishes had been knocked off in no time; handfuls of candied raisins vanished . . . Aunt Hasna was wandering around in circles, as if she suddenly didn't know what she was supposed to do anymore. And, once again, the vigilance of the negresses was circumvented. Unless the army of little runts, of beggars and homeless wretches, had—in a furious charge—forced their way through the barricade standing between them and the women feasting inside. The whole crowd that had been gathered around the gate, belligerent, threatening, showing their teeth and claws, rushed down into the wedding feast. No one knew what was happening anymore. In the wink of an eye, the house seemed to be seething; Omar was brutally thrust into a corner. The din and confusion increased, reached a climax; the guests lost their composure and were squealing frantically. Meanwhile the emaciated devils fanned out into the courtyard, into the bedrooms, the kitchen, went up onto the walkways on the first floor and invaded the terrace. The employees of the house hurried to get them out, general pandemonium followed. Imprecations rained down everywhere; the wailing of infants hovered cruelly above all the noise.

This time the confusion took a long time to dissipate.

A long, long time afterward, calm was finally restored and lasted. Then, in the newly established peaceful atmosphere, the chattering of a small kettledrum marked time to the sustained roll of a tambourine. The festivities commenced. Comings and goings subsided, the talk stopped, the groups of women broke up. As the tambourine continued in a more solemn cadence, the women—in a concerted movement—formed a circle that stretched over a large part of the courtyard.

One after the other, women singers raised their voices, each of them called out in a different manner:

Aïcha, my Lady;
Oh, my treasure,
Aïcha, my Lady,
Daughter of Bouziane . . .

The throbbing of the tambourines and the chanting that rang out freely, with no apparent cohesion or relation, soon made one's head swim.

"Zohra! On your feet. Dance, by God! You can demonstrate for all these women."

It was Aunt Hasna, thundering vehemently in that way.

A young woman, half-vexed, half-laughing, captured the attention of the guests. The women were all sumptuously attired in ample mousseline robes, in flame-colored caftans, in brocade. Their breasts were streaming with glittering jewels, gold lamé shawls were tied tightly over their hair.

"Come now," Aunt Hasna roared again. "Go ahead, my little dove! Show them!"

Other women pitched in with their entreaties, and finally the dancer consented to rise to her feet. Eyes lowered, chin pouting, she walked into the center of the large empty space in the courtyard. Raising her firm round arms, she stretched between her hands a green handkerchief which hung in front of her face; a smile roamed over her lips. Arching her torso, the young beauty began to slip imperceptibly along on her feet as her arms swung to and fro.

As for the bride, she'd been forgotten. A few relatives were sitting around her in the back of the room in the place of honor where she sat enthroned. The entire time the reveling carried on, she remained stock-still and silent, her face covered with a bride's opaque veil.

Outside, the dancer was still moving forward, swaying; a languid smile filled her eyes and her parted lips were quivering.

Shaking her head, Aunt Hasna whooped, "You've got style, little lady! A real princess, God bless me!"

Now Omar wasn't thinking of anything, could no longer remember his condition of being a starving animal. Absorbed in that vision, he forgot all the dishes; he no longer thought of the pain in his stomach, which had faded away, become remote . . . All things considered, he was happy too. He felt vaguely proud about something. Living doesn't simply mean eating, and the joy of living, simply the joy of eating.

THE COMPANION

May God protect you, good people! There is certainly no lack of affability among you! We are in the prime of life, strong and sound of mind: what more does one need? This land is far-reaching, there is room for everyone; each of us can live in his own manner, as he sees fit. Algeria, our motherland, is vast, may she be blessed! And many of our fellow countrymen are compassionate: we can testify to that before the entire universe as long as there is a breath of life left in us.

Our brothers have never let the creature that stands before you die of hunger. Hey! Everyone knows us. We are the bird that drinks from the fountain and nests in the roof tiles. Some people—most—call us Djeha, and others—friends and family—Djahdjouh.

Ah, so many rumors have gone around about ourselves! Everyone knows some story or other concerning us; the simple-minded and office clerks delight in our vicissitudes; itinerant musicians, never short on imagination, invent new ones and ascribe them to us. It is just that, God forbid, not once have I been able to hold my tongue!

Actually, I utter only truthful words to those who don't want to hear them: the merchants, the well fed, the pious, the blissful beguilers, the great who don't believe the heavens are above them, the pseudointellectuals, the ordinary when their souls are servile. I have never offended one of the poor, I swear! The poor are subjected to enough indignities as it is! I hope that will be taken into account for the sinner that I am. And if I have boasted and showed off outrageously, bah, it is simply that, deep down, I am just a silly fool.

But none of that is important. I want to tell you of a misadventure here, the latest one that your poor Djeha experienced . . .

One afternoon as I was taking my walk in town, a person whom I can still call to mind came up to me. He was dressed in an unusual fashion for the country—wearing more clothing than necessary and his attire was too dark.

"Djeha?" he asked.

"In the flesh," I confessed, and cast about trying to find the appropriate attitude to strike with the fellow.

"I know you," he said.

"Who doesn't know me, young man?"

"I know you in a different way."

Upon saying that, he shot a suggestive wink at me.

"Oh! My word . . ."

"You came out to our neighborhood one day . . . I should add that I was just a kid at the time."

"Where haven't I been, son . . . If these feet could speak!"

Nevertheless, I was growing more and more worried. I examined the man: "What is he going to come out with?" I wondered. He had sparkling eyes; they were like glowing embers. Though he was small and thin, the man, who was still young, seemed to have a good deal of innate nervous energy. As he spoke to me, his finely sculpted face crinkled up gaily and a ripple of lines furrowed his narrow, solid brow.

My scrutinizing him did not seem to bother him in the least.

He went on, "You had related your exploits to a group of neighbors who'd greatly enjoyed themselves. In compensation, one of them, Uncle Salem, had just given you a magnificent live rooster . . ."

As he pronounced these words, he was fluttering his eyelashes; I was careful. Despite an incomprehensible feeling of friendliness that was beginning to make me feel closer to him, I was not going to let myself be taken in. The boy was undoubtedly just a shameless prankster. But was it the kind smile that lit his eyes from within, or the suddenly awakened desire to find out where this fortuitous encounter was going to lead me, which subjugated me? Was there not some other, more serious explanation? I can no longer remember at all for what reason I decided to listen to him indulgently.

The answers I gave him were as reserved as possible.

"Perhaps, my good man, but I confess I can no longer recall the occasion."

Not paying the least attention to what I had said, the young man resumed.

"The group of people had dispersed. I was left alone standing next to you. I was observing you, dazed, saying to myself, 'So this is Djeha!' I would have stood there wide-eyed in front of you for a long time if at one point you hadn't glanced at me, if you hadn't motioned me to come closer and then whispered in my ear. 'Listen kid, take this rooster. Give it to your mother; have her cook it up with a good couscous.' You put the rooster in my arms and strode away."

I examined that fellow all the more closely; we struck up a conversation from there.

It didn't take long for him to confide in me and I learned that he had just arrived, that very day, from across the sea. From France! After having been away for four years, he had taken some time off to come back to see the country. And his family as well, his wife and three children. All three of them boys, he explained; the pride he felt lit a merry little flame in his eyes. However, his return had not been easy. He had been afraid of not being able to recognize them.

"Four years, my dear man, can you imagine? It stirred up awful feelings within me. I was terrified at the idea of soon finding myself before them."

Suddenly, all of my apprehensions vanished. How well I understood him! Nevertheless, he did not venture to speak to me about his wife even though he was obviously thinking of her. It is not customary in our country for a man to talk about his wife. How idiotic! Is it a crime to have a kind and pretty wife? Damn fool bunch, husbands are!

To have a comfortable talk, what could be better than sitting in front of a full teapot, is this not true? So I suggested to the young man that we go sit at the café. But he seemed quite grieved, he refused forthwith to take another step in my company. It was he who insisted on inviting me, he said, he would be very honored should I accept: he sincerely begged my pardon for not having thought of it first.

"My word, I would be delighted, if that's all it takes to make you happy!" I exclaimed.

And he calmed down. He obviously had not grasped that I had simply made the suggestion out of politeness. I did not have half a red cent to my name. It was just that everything about him had given rise to such a strong feeling of friendship that I couldn't help inviting him. For that matter, I'm sure he would have paid the bill out of respect for me.

In truth, that was not the whole story. Have you ever noticed how sometimes you are just dying to show your gratitude to others because you are feeling happy and light as a bubble? That's the way it was with that young man.

Sitting at a table in the courtyard of what used to be a fonduk, we were enjoying an excellent pot of tea. The end of the month of November was still mild. From all four corners of the building, entirely occupied by artisans, came the sound of songs and *dhikrs* (religious chants) of the babouche makers, the shrieks—like those of swallows—that the shuttles of the weavers made, the nasal cries of the hide peddlers going back and forth. Caged birds were chirping, others who were loose, answered them from atop a pomegranate tree that grew there. I immediately allowed myself to drift into the tranquillity which the clamor of the industrious hive all around me sustained.

Suddenly, my companion, who had remained silent until then, asked, "Is everything really all right in our country?"

That point-blank question gave me a start. I was not prepared for a remark of that kind coming from my friend. A bitter contrast to the reassuring sounds of everyday life all around us which had filled my heart with a delightful sensation of well-being. Tossing his curly hair, the young man, who had already told me his name was Zoubir, leaned his head toward me. I looked at him attentively: his bright eyes seemed earnest. However, it was difficult for me to guess what he was getting at.

I admitted nevertheless that, excepting myself, nothing was really all right in our country. Things were even getting worse. Without awaiting my response, he remarked, "This is what is wrong with our country: laws, lots of laws, but neither justice nor truth . . ."

Then a look as sharp as a spearhead glinted in his eyes. He spoke simply and with conviction. It was impossible not to believe that man. I listened to him. The things he said awakened a vague feeling of alarm, of uneasiness that was difficult to bear.

After a brief pause, his brow darkened.

He added, "I know it's not right to become an expatriate. If I deserted my country, do you think it was with a light heart? There was nothing else I could do. I am strong and skilled with my hands, yet I found nothing to do here."

He began to laugh. God in heaven! How delighted I was to see him in a less somber mood; his solemn eyes radiated with pure benevolence.

But he quickly began speaking again.

"I was never able to find real work. Little jobs, yes, but real work, that makes you feel satisfied once it is accomplished, never! So I left! Since then, my children have been able to eat to their heart's desire. They never see their father, but at least they have something to eat. I'm even able to save a little."

Saying that, he laughed out loud.

"Nothing spectacular," he murmured, "but at least it is something!"

I didn't understand at first why his laughter seemed so astonishing. He was young, of course! At that age, a little gaiety is enough to make all the goodness within you well up into your face. A man who at the same time works, feeds his family, and saves to boot is a wonder.

Those were the sentiments that were gradually creeping over me. I smiled at my companion; he too smiled whenever our eyes met.

I ended up assuring him, "It's quite admirable. True, you are a bit young, but you have character and you will succeed."

"I'm not sure," he responded simply.

"Love thy neighbor, among other things, but look him straight in the eye. That way, even if his intentions are not honest, he will leave you in peace."

"I am at peace with everyone, except the authorities and my father-in-law, who has a vicious tongue."

Once again, I looked at my companion in surprise.

"Such youthfulness, eh?" I thought. "Such pride, young people know what they want! Take them as an example, Djeha, you who are always getting everything mixed up and never knowing which way to go."

I felt his presence warming my heart. It was an undeserved pleasure to have such a person at my side. In my day, we did not express ourselves in that way; young people lived narrow, dreary lives, useless lives!

I can still see him as if he were standing before me. His image will never fade from my memory; I can see the greenish greatcoat he was wearing: it did not quite reach down to his knees, and it was tied at the waist with a wide belt. His small sharp-featured face was topped with a voluminous, curly mane of hair covered by neither a skullcap nor a tarboosh. His eyes shone out and cast a comforting light all around him.

Alas, sadness and joy live side by side under the same roof. After a few minutes of silence, during which it seemed as if Zoubir were calling up his entire past, he scratched his head, sighed, and began talking again, gazing out into the distance.

"You must admit, there is so much poverty in this country, one does not even know how to begin talking about it. You realize the extent of it when you come back, like I have, from a place where everyone has work, makes money, and lives happily."

Again, I felt uneasy. The self-assurance of his opinions, the maturity of the thoughts he put forth, were admittedly astonishing. But as he pronounced those words, an expression of intolerable dismay was etched upon his face. And seeing it, I felt absurdly anxious. One thing led to another and he began speaking of his father. He had been a grinder of coffee. Zoubir—yes, he upon whom life had smiled—wanted to explain to me what his father's life had been like.

"Today," he said, "wherever you go, your coffee is ground in the wink of an eye by a machine. In my childhood, that was not the case. It had to be reduced to a powder finer than the finest flour by the sole means of a man's brute strength. And that was my father's job!"

As he spoke, he clenched his fist as if it were closing over an elusive enemy. For my part, I remained silent. I did not want to hurry him while he was struggling with his memories.

"My father worked in a deep, dark cubbyhole, sort of a pit, at the end of an unpleasant blind alley. I don't know why, but the place was always closed up behind a heavy door. It looked like a prison door. You couldn't see a thing in there, it was like being buried! I remember that the pestle, made entirely of black metal, was taller than I was and weighed at least forty pounds. My father had to lift it up and bring it down endlessly, without respite all day long until it broke his back. He pounded, pounded, puffing and panting horribly. In the end, he didn't even realize what he was doing anymore. His face was drenched with abundant black sweat, streams of it glistened dimly on his forehead, his cheeks, his emaciated neck. He was already an old man; his sight was going bad and he was almost blind. His eye sockets filled with sweat as well. You would have sworn that tears were dripping from his wrinkled eyelids, and that the tears were black. There was great sadness in him, and he went on pounding, han! han! Each thud in the huge mortar tearing his chest apart."

I could not bear his story any longer, I felt overwhelmed, and yet I listened avidly. If I had not been ashamed to, I would have screamed out with pity right there among the artisans' shops, in the midst of all the bustle surrounding us. The young man was breaking my heart. "That's what our life is like," I said to myself, "and what our people are subjected to!" And sobs welled up in my throat, tightening around it like a noose.

Meanwhile the young man continued.

"Sometimes, no longer able to stay on his feet, my father would slump to the floor with his nose to the ground. I'm sure he was relieved to find himself in that position. But I was there to watch over him. I remained by his side all day long. I would immediately raise him to his feet for fear that the boss would show up and find him sprawled out on the floor. And I'd say to myself, 'You've used up all your strength, my poor father. Now all you can do is either rest or die.' I couldn't let myself feel compassion for him. I wasn't allowed to let him rest his aching limbs on the ground where they lay. He himself would have scolded and punished me afterward. I would wipe his face with a rag and, with great difficulty, pull him up and put the pestle back into his groping hands. Starting back to his work, he would whisper softly, 'Thanks, Son.' Then his strength would come back and soon the sound of his pestle could be heard pounding with a tranquil, slightly muted rhythm that shook the foundations of the old houses all around. He even started talking again; in fact, he wasn't an unhappy man. If at times he said some very bitter things, it wasn't out of unhappiness . . ."

Having gotten to that point in his tale, my friend stopped talking for a moment and his face stiffened.

Gently, I encouraged him.

"Come now, get it over with!"

He began again slowly, very slowly, upon my urging, to gather his thoughts, eyebrows raised, eyes staring straight out in front. How sorrowful he seemed! Listening to him mumbling on in that way, I felt oppressed by a strange presentiment, while at the same time a bizarre, uncontrollable, desire to reflect upon it all was growing within me. Of course that was by no means the time for considering those questions. I therefore resolved to wait for a more propitious moment.

The young voice continued, in a somewhat muffled monotone.

"When the boss would come to collect the ground coffee several times a day, he would exclaim, as if it were a joke, 'Ahmed, you're too old; you'll have to find someone to replace you.'

"At first my father would protest, saying he'd never felt better in his life; afterward he stopped answering: he seemed resigned to his fate. So, from then on, after each of the boss's appearances, I invariably overheard him grumbling, 'When I go blind, I'll become a beggar and be happier.'

"Hearing him say those words, I sincerely hoped that he would lose his sight immediately. I already pictured myself guiding him. We would have traveled many lands. That project buoyed me with hope. One day, I spoke to him about it: smiling, he answered: 'That's good. We'll go around together holding out our hands in the name of Allah.'

"Things didn't turn out the way we'd planned; my father expired with his hands clutching the pestle."

The young man fell silent as if some invisible thing had suddenly frightened him; his features quivered and his whole face tensed. He bowed his head, sat there motionless. He seemed to be listening for something. After some time, he nodded his head.

Just when I was least expecting it, he finished his tale with these words, "It was at the end of the day that it would become terrifying. He would let out such atrocious screams of pain, it was unbearable. It was late then; I'd run to call for mama and together, holding him up under each arm, we'd drag him to the house."

I too recall a grim, meager existence. It was tedious, a feeling of lassitude that gripped one's soul hung over it like a sleepy haze. It was so tedious, you felt you were suffocating: it was a flow of lead running into one's lungs. When I call up that still recent past, I find it difficult to believe that was the way things really were. It's true, men were enveloped in a shroud of ignorance and fear. They walked around with their heads bowed; cringing, they dared not show themselves. But today? Today, look at how they have learned to respect themselves. To refuse being humiliated. We have lifted the veil of grief that was tied around our hearts. May God bestow long life upon us all, and we will see better days. Djeha says so! When that time comes, things will go wrong only for those who have a guilty conscience.

To come back to the man sitting in front of me, there he was, happy once again, father of three boys, holding a job . . .

The two of us were sitting there talking. You would have thought he'd just lived through a long nightmare in those few minutes; he closed his eyes and, as if overwhelmed with remorse, wondered, "What came over me, letting myself get drawn into those memories?"

He seemed completely despondent. Then he opened his eyes again: his gaze was lit with a kind smile.

It was in that same second that I glimpsed dark groups of

policemen rushing into the fonduk and swooping down around us like a swarm of vultures. And what can I say, friends? Had we been struck by some disaster? I didn't know what was happening anymore. Dear God, brothers, it was horrific! They all laid into us. Blows rained down. Those killers charged on us, iron helmets covering their heads down to the ears. We were hit in the belly, on the legs, on the back. Several people were running with bloodied mouths, others, with their heads split open. Turbans went flying off the heads of honorable fellow citizens; peaceful artisans were scattered, trampled upon; the others, me, and my companion, all of us were arrested and chained up in the wink of an eye like so many crooks. And for what reason, God almighty? But I was only to learn the reason later, when I was released from prison.

Zoubir recovered right away. After what had just happened, bullied by those cops drunk with brutality, it was difficult to get a grip on one's self again, to tell the truth. In any case, I was dazed. The good young man was actually addressing me very calmly.

"There you are! Ah, is that you? Don't worry, it's all over . . ."

It was all over? I remained silent, taciturn; I was not as sure as he was. My heart was pounding wildly; in there, alarming warning signals were raising an uncustomary, remote but clearly perceptible racket. Even so, in my confused state, though there was no reason for me to rejoice, I was at least happy about one thing: having found my companion again. You can't imagine how much difference a familiar face can make in those circumstances. Gradually, I began to regain confidence. But, bless me, gentlemen, what a scuffle! From fear or surprise, I'm not sure which, my back was nevertheless drenched. It could well have been from fear, come to think of it.

But we were then going to go across town, right out in plain sight of our population, oh shame . . . I bowed down, kept quiet, and walked . . . Seeing me so downcast, Zoubir questioned me in a low voice, as the other captives followed and preceded us.

"Are you afraid?"

"No."

"Indeed, there's no reason to be."

Just then a strange idea occurred to me. "The owner of the café," I thought to myself, "he served us his tea being unaware of what was going to happen. Who will pay him, pay for his glasses, his tables and chairs, his busted, broken benches?" I pictured him lamenting over the wretched remains of his property and, forgive me, I couldn't hold back a laugh which suddenly shook me. Why? It would be quite difficult for me to explain. As the saying goes, "Joy and sorrow are next-door neighbors."

That was when I noticed him, walking along up front, ahead of us, it was him all right, without his turban, which he must have lost in the fray! At first glance, I recognized that massive rugged Kalmuck head, shaved clean, reaching down to the neck in thick folds covered with prickly hairs. The owner of the café was walking in such a dignified manner, one would have thought he was accompanying a nuptial convoy: chin uplifted, as if it were he who was showing the way to the police. "Upon my word as Djeha!" I said to myself then. "I must show as much dignity as my brother, my demeanor must absolutely appear to be as imposing as his." I swelled my chest, furrowed my brow, and went forward swinging my arms, like an official of some sort. I instantly felt as if I had grown taller, as if I were higher up than usual. At that moment I was thinking, "We'll go and see *their* prison. What's wrong with that? Men are meant to be imprisoned as well."

Feeling reinvigorated, I was moving along comforted by those thoughts when, from the crowd of onlookers who gathered as we passed and gazed at us in respect, a European jumped out and rushed up to us. He was foaming at the mouth; he was screaming.

Lifting up his clenched fist, he vociferated, "Stop!"

Then that animal started lashing out and braying as if he had lost his mind. And no one understood why it was my young companion who received all the blows. Zoubir was jumping from side to side trying to escape them; he made an attempt at defending himself, but the handcuffs bound his wrists together.

"Hold him back! Whoa! For pity's sake, hold him back!"

No one among the police officers who stood watching even raised an eyebrow. From the crowd of curious onlookers, some murmurs arose. Was someone going to save us from that raving madman or not? The police officers aimed their guns, on one side at us, and on the other at the crowd. The crowd fell silent, remained still. So it was at that moment that I became frightened, was seized with irrational panic. The European, protected by the pistols, continued clubbing our friend. I was observing myself and everything around me as if I had somehow been unbelievably split in two; however I cannot confirm that I had not completely lost my senses. Suddenly Zoubir let out a groan: a weak and horrific sound, the sound made by a branch when it breaks. He shook his chained hands in the air, arched backward, and fell to the ground, dragging me down along with him in his fall. His whole body was quivering but he did not let out a cry. Arching his back more and more, he craned out his neck and goggled one eye at me: it held a glint of insanity so ghastly that no human tongue could express it. Then his head fell back down. I was lying almost flat on the ground next to him.

The other man went on kicking him with his boots.

"Bastard! Do you think I'm going to let you live?" he shouted.

Brothers, I never thought a man's heart could contain so much hatred. On that day, I saw what your eyes would refuse to believe. Lord, preserve us from that madness, silence that voice within us.

I would be lying to you if I told you how we were able to continue our march: from that moment onward, the events that followed become unraveled, grow blurry in my mind. Just as certain isolated things have been etched in my memory with disquieting precision, certain others drift around in a roiling, unpredictable fog. Thus I only partially recall how it was that we got to our feet, and in what condition we, the prisoners, continued as best we could along our way, holding our companion up . . .

The way that was to lead us to prison. Pain had clutched onto my shoulders like a wild beast. Dazed, I was dragging myself along, tormented by the sound the bones of my friend had made; his wrinkled and dust-covered suit now looked like a sack. Also, the fine flame of fraternity I'd felt for mankind had been snuffed out; I was roaming about in unfathomable darkness. Zoubir's head lolled this way and that on his chest, his back slumped inward, his arms dangled; he wasn't walking, we were simply carrying him.

After that, I am not really sure what happened. When I came to, my whole body ached. I was soaking wet, as if several buckets of dirty, nauseating water had been thrown on me. My head was swollen, heavy: it was still filled with a tremendous racket. I didn't feel like saying anything, seeing anything: everything seemed so odious to me. A great number of strangers were piled up with us in a long narrow cell; everyone remained sprawled out motionless, like felled tree trunks; some still found the strength to moan. I waited; I was listening to the sound of water sloshing not far from there. Lying flat on my back I observed my surroundings, not understanding, my mind reeling. After a few seconds, I was able to make out I'm not sure which grizzled, gray faces, flat on the cement. Somewhere, in a corner, or on the other side of a wall—but where exactly?—someone was watching. Yet I could not see anyone. It was as if a face hidden in the half-light had its eyes turned on me and was rolling them around; I had a tremendous urge to raise myself up, despite the strange weakness that filled my limbs, in order to better study it. But rooted to the spot, I could no longer move, not even lift an arm. Suddenly I was seized with an irresistible urge to flee. Then I was able to fully realize the monstrosity of the situation in which I found myself; my mind suddenly grew clearer and I thought, "Djeha, Djeha, what's happening to you? What have you gotten yourself into? Poor devil!"

I could not resist the impulse urging me to rise immediately. Yet I had hardly reached a sitting position when a long howling sound pulled me out of my torpor with a start. I glanced about with crazed eyes. It wasn't coming from our cell: it was bizarre! In any case it so startled me, I fell over flat on the floor, spent, close to losing consciousness. In my semiconscious state, I realized there were also prisoners on the other side of the wall. In the same instant, a door closed, making the dark heavy building shake, the sound of dragging footsteps echoed in the hallway, and a long rattling breath crossed the silence. I was huddled up in my corner. The same sounds were repeated, came flooding through the house again like a wave. From then on, a pained and rhythmical plaint hung over the close rattling breathing, which drew out for long minutes until it had completely spent itself. Lying on my belly, I listened, gasping, I was staring at something straight in front of me, and what I saw then almost made me lose my mind.

There, on the floor, lay Zoubir, facing skyward; his fists, clenched over his thumbs, were resting on his chest. His now dull eyes looked like congealed fat. However, his eyebrows were raised very high as if he were relating the sad story of his father again to an invisible listener. That empty gaze stubbornly fixed on the blurred white of the ceiling was beginning to seem rather odd. Then I noticed his mouth hanging open; from the corners of his blackened lips, trickles of brown-colored blood ran along his cheeks and around his neck. The blood had formed a dark puddle under the young man's head. Zoubir was not moving. The blood flowed imperceptibly from him without cease: one would have thought my friend was melting. Suddenly the room grew very cold, and I was particularly horror-stricken. Jaws clenched, I started to go numb.

Later, much later on, it seemed to me, I realized that I was not in the same place: the atmosphere in which I found myself was completely different. I was in a well-lit, spacious room, with other people of course. My companion had disappeared; no more signs of blood on the floor.

What had become of him? I asked the people around me, none of them could answer; some did not even understand what I was talking about. And it is possible that they took me for someone who had been deranged by all the recent events.

I could tell by the look on their faces that they seemed to pity me. That was only the beginning!

However, I did learn that we were going to be interrogated: that is what we had been prepared and brought there for. In fact, a powerful voice began calling names out immediately: they were to be the first to be brought before the authorities.

When my turn finally came and I stepped forward, a man who was sitting behind a desk began grumbling, shaking his head.

He then exclaimed, "Dja-kha! Djo-kha! Another name that's impossible to pronounce! What's this guy doing here? And daffy to boot! Go on, get a move on!"

Upon those last words, which he had spit in my face, he lifted his eyes toward me. What an expression, the look in his eyes! He was only human, just as we are, you might remark. Yet if everyone were like him, there'd be cause to have fear of and for mankind.

Those thoughts, which were far from gay, were rolling around in my mind, and I had forgotten the presence of the representative of law and order, it all seemed so horrific to me. Suddenly someone grabbed me by the collar, pushed me unceremoniously toward the door, and once there, I received a kick smack between the buttocks. The police agent who threw me out in that manner must have had a lot of practice in treating people that way.

As if by enchantment, I was once again in the street, amid the endless comings and goings of passersby, of citizens going about their business, itinerant merchants whose repeated calls echoed out from one street to another, children larking around like impudent swallows, cars speeding along, paying no heed to pedestrians. I sank into the surging crowd, was swept away in it, amid thousands of cries, thousands of sounds, furious bicycle bells, heady songs expectorated by gramophones in the cafés, the voices of donkey drivers shouting themselves hoarse: "*Balek! Balek!*" the hammering of all the cobblers set up out in the open. Finding myself mixed in with human beings, hearing all that free, carefree life, filling my lungs with fresh air without paying a cent, feeling God's good sun shining on my back even though winter was imminent, well er—must I confess?—I did not feel joyful or satisfied.

Was I not free? Was I not like those ringdoves I saw hopping about this way and that on the pavement, pecking here and there, then—suddenly frightened—flushing up into the air where they wheeled around so gracefully one never tired of admiring them? Was I not also going to go back to my previous life, and like those birds "drink from the fountain and nest in the roof tiles"? I was not sure. I was no longer sure.

I certainly was not in the least inclined to take up my old habits again, and the idea didn't even dawn on me. No, I did not feel free yet! I am incapable of explaining what was happening to me, but that is exactly how I felt. I still had the feeling I was down in my dark dungeon, crammed in with my companions of misfortune to the point of smothering. It was as if I were carrying my prison on my back with me out in those streets, or that my soul had been thrown into prison too, and it was still there, whereas I was walking around unfettered out in the wide world.

I roamed the city; and disjointed ideas, lugubrious ideas jostled one another, crowded into my ravaged brain. Honest people who saw me passing by and all the numerous—praise God—folk who still remembered their good friend Djeha and addressed him with many greetings, seeing they were ignored, shook their heads sadly. One of them sighed loudly enough for me to hear him. "That's what prison brings!" Ah! How well that man understood me!

I wandered around for a long time in that state of mind. How many hours? Who could say? The dense, suffocating heat of that cloudless November weighed upon the city. The image of my dead companion floated in front of me, his blood once again streaming out before my eyes. There was something welling up larger and larger in my head or in my heart . . . It had all happened because, as I had learned a few minutes before being booted out of prison, all of that because some freedom fighters had risen up to defend their land. And then a strange calm fell over me, my mind fell cold again. A feeling of lucidity, of incredible strength, a sort of enthusiasm, like a great swelling song, filled my soul. Our brothers out there in the mountains—had they finally taken up arms against the vermin devouring us from within? But what do you think will happen now? Each day will see new freedom fighters join them!

THE LONG WAIT

That afternoon when Omar returned from his wanderings, the room was bathed with a shimmering glow. The light that spread through the room or that suddenly shot through it created an atmosphere as hard and compact as steel. Aouicha and Mériem, drenched with sweat and lying side by side on the bare tile floor, were asleep, or pretending to be asleep.

When she heard her brother come in, Aouicha raised herself up. She remained in a seated position, leaning on one arm. She stared at him without moving, her eyes trailing after who knows what demented thought. Despair could be seen in them: Omar stood stock-still.

He was watching her; little by little Aouicha seemed to begin seeing him. With a toss of her head, she motioned toward the dish in which bits of bread floated. Omar squatted down. With his fingers, he fished out the crumbs—white as milk—that were soaking in the saucer filled with water.

Afterward, he gulped down the remaining liquid in deep swallows.

In that instant, Aouicha darted a fierce glance at him.

"Were you out begging again?"

"I swear . . ."

"Stop lying. I saw you going into Yamina's."

"I swear I refused to take the figs she wanted to give me."

"You hang around the neighbor's doors a bit too much."

"I'd just run an errand for her."

"Next time, tell her to run her own errands! When Ma comes back, I'm going to tell her everything."

"But I'm telling you . . ."

When she had departed for Oujda, their mother had left Aouicha, the eldest of the children, with only a few francs.

But the money never lasted long; the sum had barely sufficed to cover their food for one day. And from the next day on, it was up to God's graces. They had subsisted as well as they could, fixing up some old leftovers here, borrowing a few cents there.

Three days had gone by; Aïni still did not come back from her journey.

Omar had thought about those *journeys* of hers several times. Since war had been declared, contraband had once again become a prosperous enterprise, which no one would ever have predicted. His mother, who had thought she would never return to Oujda, began smuggling Moroccan textiles into the country again. Now Omar simply considered these absences to be difficult periods to get through. Undeniably, following each of them, an era of abundance—although short-lived—would begin. Everything was fine for a few days. And later, everything went back to the way it was before!

In the meantime, he would stop, in spite of himself, in the doorways of the other rooms, without making himself too obvious. He watched the neighbors setting up their meïdas. At times someone would call out to him, offer him a tidbit. Rarely did he accept, but rather would refuse embarrassedly and flee.

On the fourth day, night was once again falling without Aïni having come home. The children gave up waiting for her and put their hopes off until the next day.

Ever since their mother had left, the hours, the days stretched out with frightening slowness. There were long moments when not a word escaped their lips.

During the day, they would wander around, tense and restless. At the house, the tenants, who secretly watched their worried faces, called out to them from time to time.

"Your mother has abandoned you! You'll never see her again!"

The children knew they were wicked gossips.

"Who knows? Maybe she's found a husband?" the women scoffed. "If that's the case, she'll never come back."

Their mother . . . How ridiculous. Why make jokes that

made it even harder for them? They were devastated enough as it was . . .

Even the landlady! Now that their mother was gone, she would spout off the wickedest things; she trumpeted to all who would listen.

"Why did that heartless woman leave, abandoning her children, leaving them to die of hunger? Why? Boo! How can one do such a thing?"

She was beginning to feel pity for them, that old hag! A woman whose dried-up bosom was forever filled with hate.

Between two venomous diatribes, she would stop and laugh ecstatically.

"Hee! Hee! Hee!"

What ghastly merriment!

A heavy but vague agony was stirring in Omar. Confiding in his older sister, he told her almost in a whisper that hunger was torturing him. Aouicha remained silent.

She just kept repeating the same thing to him.

"Oumima will come today, I'm sure of it. She'll arrive this evening."

She had been saying the same thing since Aïni had left!

Aouicha withdrew into a corner; the boy walked away with a heavy heart. He could tell his sister resented her mother and everyone else.

That is why she started treating them, Mériem and himself, harshly.

"What do you want me to do?" she would cry out suddenly. "She's gone, she abandoned you."

Then she would protest, "Am I hiding money somewhere? She only left for two days. And now four days have gone by!"

She would invariably end up screaming, "I can't do anything about it! I can't do anything! You're driving me crazy!"

The afternoon of the fifth day they were waiting with clenched teeth. They had stretched themselves out across the floor of the room. They were besieged by blasts of early August heat radiating through their bodies, making their temples pulse painfully. Everything was turning bright vermillion before their eyes. The air was streaked with veins of fire. From then on, they trembled constantly with fever. They found it difficult to rise to their feet; in spite of the thirst strangling them, they had no desire to drink; it was hunger.

Aouicha, whom anger had driven to distraction, sat off at a distance and observed them, shaking her head. She forbade them to complain; their moaning irritated her. It wasn't their fault? Too bad! They were to keep their mouths shut! Her suffering had made her cruel. Suddenly, sobs shook her. Her weeping, which she had tried to hide, immediately made her eyes puff up and all expression drained from them.

Daylight was slowly waning, lending a chalky cast to the air; that most sullen time of day overwhelmed the children. They had reached the limit of their resistance, after which despair sets in.

Along with the sun, the slightest sign of a breeze had vanished from the air. A dryness like that of dead ashes hung over the house. The children shivered with fever.

They lay down beside one another and fell asleep as if in a dark incubator.

The next day, the sun—Omar would never forget it—rose copper colored. In an ominous sky, trails of clouds scudded away on a wind that could not yet be felt. The sirocco was coming. They couldn't hope to have anything to eat that morning either. They splashed well water on their faces to cool themselves off. And the long wait started in again.

Four o'clock in the afternoon. It was the time their older sister had said their mother's train arrived. After that, no use in counting on her coming back.

Omar was calm, but he certainly wasn't as imperturbable as Mériem. His little sister didn't seem to feel anything, not the hunger or the heat—thick enough to cut with a knife—or the torturous wait . . . Sitting on the doorstep, she had a piece of wood in her mouth that she was sucking on with placid satisfaction. A little bit of yellow spittle had dried at the corners of her mouth. Her face remained closed.

Aouicha was, indubitably, the most jittery; her aloofness was just a show. Her irritation was vibrating, hidden, terrifying.

Omar was sitting cross-legged in the middle of the room, his head leaning on one shoulder. Fascinated with Mériem's face, he was soon under the illusion that he was looking at an old woman, or rather a woman who had grown old in the wink of an eye. Suddenly his sister was several hundred years old, while her features remained those of a little girl.

Just then, a strange commotion spread through Dar Sbitar. The two girls, Aouicha and Mériem, rushed toward the stairway. Omar recognized his mother's voice among those of the other women. He had no desire to get to his feet. The neighbor women greeted Aïni with surprised cries, shrill exclamations, laughter, questions . . .

Still sitting in the same place, Omar slumped over on himself with all his weight. He heard his mother's voice again.

He loathed that sound. It jarred his nerves, its contact now tore him apart. Suddenly he felt a frantic need to despise everything and to disappear. That was understandable, what with that loathing. But before sinking into it forever, before being completely engulfed in it, he huddled himself up at the highest point of his suffering. He fell silent in order to listen to the collapse.

Then, from an almost numb rage, the first small openings of pain formed. In the meantime, he was counting on making himself as inert as a corpse. His hatred, his hatred, what was he going to do about it? Wasn't she going to stand by him anymore? He had no other arms in which to seek refuge: it wouldn't have been any different anywhere else, this prison wouldn't change; suffering would be the same everywhere. He wished, with every particle of his child's soul, he could dissolve. In that same instant, deep in the recesses where his thoughts were formulating that wish, he was gripped by sheer panic. Tears came slowly rolling down his tense face.

THE ENCHANTED HEIR

I thank the stars for having showered favors upon me. My beloved parents left me a vast house . . . I also received land from them. This affluence insulated my life against the hard knocks of adversity for all time. I've become the master of the wooded peaks that surround our home. (Beyond them stretch pasturelands as well, rolling down all the way to the plain.)

Yet it's nothing compared to what we once possessed. All that is left us now are mere crumbs. It must date a long way back; I descend from a renowned family; I am their last representative . . . Their succession falls to me now. I wasn't at all familiar with these domains which have now been handed over to me. I am no more familiar with them now that they are mine. Not once has the idea to go out and inspect them occurred to me. I suppose that might seem odd. My personal occupations have always diverted my attention!

The same tragedy that deprived me of my parents forced me at the time to take charge of it all. Never have I been given such prodigious cause for worry as back in those distant days. What was I to do? What was to become of me? I was panic-stricken just at the thought of having to manage such vast domains, having had no other experience but that of living a carefree life. I had never worked any kind of a job; true, I had gone to school when I was an adolescent. But that was so long ago!

Those day-to-day tasks, the problems, were a humiliation to me; thus I spent whole days feeling completely at a loss. I thought I would have to roll up my sleeves and dig in! I saw people throng into my house, presenting themselves as tenant farmers, forest rangers, *khammès* (sharecroppers), head shepherds, leaseholders . . . They told me how afflicted they were. The death of my parents was evidently at the root of their affliction. They solemnly swore fidelity to me. Then they provided me with the accounts of their farms and all their activities. I trusted them about everything and they returned to their homes with the assurance of my protection, which they had all hoped to obtain.

It was only then that I realized that everything was continuing as it had in the past. My intervention in my own affairs proved completely unnecessary. I calmed down. I understood that what was needed above all was a master. I was that master. And life went on as usual. I never had to worry about protecting my interests again. Today I laugh about my apprehensions, which seem ridiculous now. However, a vague feeling of commiseration for my people was dawning in my conscience; yes, to see them accept that this was the way things were.

I had just discovered that superior and natural order established by our first ancestors. It continued to function without my participation being necessary. It controlled itself, so that everything was accomplished as if under the supervision of the master. But didn't it all come down to the same thing in the end?

Once again, my only guide was my liberty. My ambition was to attain an enlightened life, free of the dreary yoke of daily toil, the prison of labor that entraps human existence. Far from any sacrilegious attack, that ideal burned like a flame after which I was forever chasing.

The assets that happened to be in my possession did not fail to fructify, and I married. Though I am only thirty years old, I now have two children.

Nevertheless, of all the things I possess, I can say that nothing is dearer to me than our house. It is tied to my heart with secret binds. This house which we inhabit alone, my wife, my children, and myself—however, can I still say, "I live in my house"? Similarly, can I say, "My wife, my children"?—rises from amid a wood of cork oaks. I wouldn't be able to give a detailed description of it; it is so vast that it's impossible to evoke even an approximate idea. I've never been able to take in its overall exterior appearance, and from the inside it's just a series of rooms: walking through such immense rooms, it's difficult to believe it's merely a house. Actually, my wife, my children, and I live in a palace! These chambers had been designed on such a scale that I believe I'm correct in thinking that each one of them was once intended to house an entire family. To be more exact, I must add that nothing absolute separates them. They stretch on endlessly; one only notices he is passing from one to the other owing to certain architectural details. Therefore it would have been ridiculous to try to furnish or decorate such a residence. That is why I have always kept the few pieces of furniture that had been placed here and there by my ancestors. My wife and I have refrained from changing the slightest thing about it, from moving the smallest object! Was it necessary? Was it even wise? We were happy just to live there, modeling ourselves after our forefathers. They themselves had already lived there, just as their predecessors had!

I thank the stars for having showered favors upon me: never have I sought to learn the reasons for those favors. On the contrary, I have taken great care not to delve into their purposes. Attempts of that kind are always vain. Venture into the labyrinth of causes I could never know, what for? Wouldn't that be prideful? It would be wanting to disturb the order of the world, undermine something that is greater than we are. Wouldn't it be wiser to enjoy the wealth that Providence has granted us? When destiny decides to smile upon you, it all happens very quickly; there's no way of knowing how it happened. And what it has bestowed upon you, no one will take from you. Then there's nothing left to do but thank the stars. In the same way, if it decides to disinherit you, that too occurs very quickly. And you still have to thank the stars. Because nothing depends on you, not even your life. May the rich be rich and the poor, poor, since nothing originates with us.

I wasn't despondent about the death of my parents for long. I'd already glimpsed the grandeur of our tradition, which shielded me from despair. From that moment on, I understood that our true destiny consists, not in conserving our possessions—which, all the way back to our remotest relatives, have been perpetuated until they reached us—but, for me and my children, in transmitting our tradition to those who will follow us. Our task was set out for us; possessions in this world are only the ties that our lives maintain with the parental powers.

In my family we have always scrupulously followed the dictates that our forefathers have bequeathed to us from time immemorial. Generations have risen up one after the other and disappeared; we will nonetheless continue to model our lives on that precept. Our lives could be snuffed out without leaving a trace, yet the continuity of our tradition would not be affected in any way whatsoever.

I enjoyed wandering through the woods around our home at daybreak. I would breathe in the acrid smell of freshly turned earth, where trees had recently been uprooted, and the gentler smell of the wet leaves strewn on the ground. Those living fragrances came wafting through the moist air. Though the sun wasn't up yet, there was a sharp cast to the morning light. Susceptible to the magic that exudes from the things of nature, I would be filled with unmitigated bliss. My soul, charged with the mysterious influence of so moving and so simple a moment, was jubilantly savoring the familiar magnificence of the scene.

One's heart is filled with contentment at such times. The calm hour, the newborn light playing between the trees, everything tended to draw my thoughts into deep reverie. Listening to the birdsong rising from branch to branch, I allowed my eyes to rove through the timberland, and felt that time of day to be the most serene of all.

That day I went out as usual in the early morning and walked out among the trees. I remember even the slightest details about that moment, which I've so often called to mind. My spirit was at peace in the joy which that ineffable exuberance perpetuated on earth. Little by little, a feeling of tranquillity began to creep into me. The kind of tranquillity that a human heart is usually never given to experience. It was in that very instant that I heard the voices of several men echoing in the underbrush. They had just torn me abruptly out of that frame of mind which was like a state of contemplation. I stopped and briefly deliberated with myself, having determined to take a different path than the one on which I had started out. My aim was to avoid meeting people I didn't know. Or, if by chance I did know them, not to reveal my presence to them. However, as I was moving forward, intending to take a different direction, I found myself facing, though at some distance, Si Adar. He was with two other people. I couldn't pretend that I hadn't recognized him, because he smiled at me immediately. The three of them stood at the end of a line of trees; their silhouettes outlined clearly against the sky.

From the way Si Adar was smiling at me, I understood that the conversation that was keeping him in the company of the two men was drawing to an end. I therefore began to walk over toward the group.

They were talking about a laborer, previously employed by one of Si Adar's friends, whom they felt was a discontented troublemaker. Their unspoken fear was that if they kept him on, he would contaminate other laborers. They demanded only diligence and honesty of their ordinary laborers, convinced they made good subjects of them in that way. Whereas in handpicked subjects, such as the fellah in question, they feared precisely curiosity, pride, audaciousness.

"Submission," Si Adar was saying, "that's something he could never conceive of! And yet that idea must be first and foremost in everyone's minds. I wouldn't hesitate to declare that the concept comes straight from God, and is, in a manner of speaking, the most powerful expression of his presence among men."

He turned his inexpressive and dark eyes on me.

"What's lacking today," he sighed, "is neither knowledge nor intelligence, but rather being satisfied with one's lot."

"They're encouraged by the government that's just emerged from the war," Mr. Valé added. "Their boldness will know no limits now. But we'll be able to make them see reason. Algeria is not France."

Si Adar was a tall man, with steady eyes, wearing a European-style suit of gray cloth. He carried his handsome elongated head, creased with age, tilted slightly toward his right shoulder. His bold traits expressed, paradoxically, the dignity and shrewdness undoubtedly acquired in his frequent relations with others.

It was quite a strange experience, listening to him speak. He expressed himself in very correct French. His speech was more elegant than that of his interlocutor, Mr. Valé. I even think that, though he was Arab, Si Adar was utterly convinced that he expressed himself more flawlessly than did the Frenchman.

He soon left his friends. Si Adar and I saw each other fairly often. But that didn't keep us from greeting one another with lively and profuse salutations whenever we met. When one encounters a friend again after an hour's absence, isn't it as if he were coming back from afar? After having shaken his hand, asked after his family, in conclusion I wished him good health. He did the same for me in turn. After that he suggested we go for a ride in his car.

"Since," as he said, "we've had the good fortune of encountering one another today."

Talking all the while, we reached the main road where his car was parked. I often had the opportunity to go on hikes with him in the country. Sitting up front in the automobile, we soon found ourselves driving through the woods.

From time to time we came out on deserted fields, over which a light mist hung. There, out in plain daylight, we were confronted with the gloomy life of labor and misery led by the fellahs, men who were devoured by weakness and timidity.

We soon reached a spot where there was a sort of inn. We could stop there and even have something to drink. At any rate, it was impossible for me to stay away from the house for long. We stopped at the inn. As he walked in, Si Adar was happy to encounter another of his friends, whom he immediately invited to sit at our table. And scarcely had he struck up a conversation with him than he seemed impassioned. I was only listening to them distractedly. The sound of their voices reached me through a screen of thoughts. I was thinking of my wife and children, who were alone. Ah! No question of hanging around there very long. "Guests might come to my house at any minute," I said to myself. "Who will welcome them in my place? Would my wife do it for me? But it's not customary for a woman to welcome guests. And my guests, would they find it fitting? If I am the master of the domain, and strangers come to my house, it's my duty to greet them." Those were the questions I was debating in my mind while Si Adar, particularly absorbed in his discussion, went on endlessly talking and laughing discreetly.

I'm not sure anymore how I was able to leave that place. On the other hand I do recall that the reason that drove me to do so was real.

"I'll be right back," I'd said to Si Adar as I went out.

I was far from thinking at the time that I was going to go home. A path, a shortcut, leading away from the inn, went straight to the house. The path wasn't often used; to be exact, I couldn't remember ever having taken it. I even wonder how I had become convinced that it existed. I don't recall either that anyone ever spoke of it in my presence. Yet I was persuaded that a path of that sort was to be found there. That conviction was deeply rooted in my mind. I felt capable of somehow reinventing, step-by-step, the trajectory I was going to follow. Lost in those thoughts, I found myself imperceptibly drawn in a direction that finally seemed to be the one I was looking for. I had been so anticipating that discovery that it didn't surprise me.

As I moved forward, the woods grew denser; but the feeling that I was nearing the house grew stronger. Soon there was nothing but thick undergrowth imprisoning the path. The narrow, sinuous trail dwindled until it seemed to come to an end. As I made my way through the cork oaks, impatient as I was to get home, a feeling of extreme anxiety crept over me. Then I began dashing about like a madman. At times I urged myself to press on in the same direction, the only one that could be taken, at others, filled with regrets, I decided to go back the way I'd come. I vacillated back and forth in that way without being able to make up my mind which solution to adopt. In fact, instead of looking for a way out of that labyrinth, I was trying to go deeper in, convinced of being on the right track.

The path was in every way identical to the one I had imagined. I would soon reach the house, there was no doubt of it. Though out of breath—my thoughts were so confused that, to tell the truth, they prevented me from feeling how fatigued I was—I ran even farther than I had up to that point. But why did I have the feeling that misfortune was weighing an imminent threat down upon me in that solitude?

I was becoming more and more persuaded that I would never find the path leading home, it seemed as if I would never escape that prison of trees. My apprehension was growing and became so intense that it turned into anxiety, which enhanced the feeling that a danger was threatening my family while I was wandering around far from them.

It was then that my curiosity was aroused by the vision of several female forms: I turned my head away; my eyes were drawn involuntarily in their direction. There were only three of them, and one—judging by appearances—was but an old woman. However, she had such a casual tilt to her head, she was so sprightly in her movements, one would have thought she was as young as the other two. They appeared to be fleeing or pursuing one another through the trees. All three were staring at me. When I looked more closely, I noticed that their eye sockets were empty. Dressed in very wispy, pale-colored fabrics, they moved along very slowly, then all at once very rapidly. Just when I would have sworn they were far from me, I discovered them by my side.

Here I realize that I must interrupt this tale long enough to note a detail that is bound to cause surprise, even though—all things considered—it is something of very little importance.

While I was staring, with quite understandable perplexity, at the three strange creatures, a great number of rats began to flee. They were all black; their bloodshot eyes were so bright and filled with mischief that one would have thought they were the eyes of humans who'd been thus transformed. They weren't exactly fleeing, even when I approached, but scurrying around aimlessly. It wasn't only that they didn't seem to fear me in the least, but they appeared to be mocking me and even darting insolent looks in my direction. They never tired of performing countless somersaults that seemed somehow cruel. In my haste, I unintentionally crushed one of them underfoot.

Then I realized that the three women were going to pounce on me because they had all three surrounded me in a concerted movement. All of that took place in a most extraordinary silence. I miraculously escaped them and recalled I had a pistol in a pocket of my jacket. I immediately brandished it, counting on the fear that a firearm is likely to inspire.

In the same instant, I noticed that each of the women was holding a pistol exactly like my own in her hand. Having thus become convinced that they had decided to kill me, I didn't hesitate, and shot at the oldest one, who seemed to control the others. But what happened, which I had no way of foreseeing, was this: in the instant I pulled the trigger, I heard no detonation. Yet I'm certain that several shots were fired. The women too had fired on me. Luckily I hadn't been hit, at least I hadn't felt any pain; but was that proof enough? I charged on, having cast my weapon to one side. Finally, I arrived at my house. Though there was nothing before me but an immense wall, I lost no time in locating a large door which had been bricked up. The newer masonry work began two feet from the ground. That particularly odd detail, which I saw as the manifestation of some auspicious design—perhaps it was simply the result of inexplicable negligence—was familiar to me. Yet I'm not sure I had ever seen it before. I dove into that passageway and found myself in a sort of large vestibule. It was very dark; however, at the back an opening similar to the first had been made. From that, I calculated that the gallery must not be very long. Having crouched down again, I went through the second opening and suddenly came out in our house. I was in the common room.

My wife was standing in front of me, back turned, feeding the children. Upon seeing that scene my heart brimmed up with a feeling of such exultation it frightened me. I spoke mentally to her ineffable presence. Words of silence cropped up in my memory: "I don't know how to say thank you. You shield my life from all threats. It took me a long time to realize that. Forgive me, my love!"

No one had heard me come in; I drew slowly nearer to my

wife until I could have touched her. I noticed she wasn't paying any attention to me; she continued feeding her children as if she hadn't remarked my presence. They, whose brows I could have touched in stretching out my arm, didn't see me. They remained impervious to everything but their meal. Usually, no matter what their mother did to calm them, they would greet me with loud shouts. Now they weren't even aware I was there.

My gentle wife was thoroughly absorbed with them. One would have thought that she was closed over some inner conviction that fulfilled her. Her hand reaching toward the children revealed the line of her breast under her massive mane of hair. Such carelessness in my presence prevented me from even so much as brushing against her. And the unaccustomed gravity that I noted in her gestures made me feel estranged from her.

The sound of voices came from the next room. I went in that direction and found myself in front of three people I knew. They were friends whom I had invited to come and spend the day at the house. But I did not see the slightest thing in their manner either to indicate that I existed. They were talking calmly among themselves.

I didn't dare speak to my friends anymore than I had to my wife. I couldn't admonish them, even jokingly, for their indifference. Some subliminal warning dissuaded me from doing so. It was impossible for me to question them, as I knew it entailed a certain risk. My only hope lay in Si Adar, whom I had just left. He was the man for the circumstances, I had to find him at all costs. I had to act immediately if I wanted to prevent some unfortunate event from occurring. My salvation depended upon it.

That evening, I'd just come home, I'd been out combing the countryside in vain. For the last few minutes long processions of women had been following one after the other to our room. Once at the door, they stopped, looked inside, and remained on the threshold. Some had shawls framing their faces. Many of them were covering their mouths with their hands.

"Enough, enough!" some were saying. "What use is it to weep like that? May God's will be done."

Others were shaking their heads vigorously, looking sad and dejected.

"He is now in the presence of God," said one of them.

A voice, strangled with sobs, came from the back of the room. It was that of my wife.

"I'm but a poor woman. Why do I keep on living? Cursed be this day."

The death lament rose, high-pitched, as if it should never stop. Suddenly it fell to a sort of hoarse moaning.

"Who will stand by me now?" she went on. "I have lost the one to whom I could turn my eyes."

Several women were sobbing at the same time.

"Have I only lived to see the one who was my very life depart? Lord, how miserable I am!"

A few women, slapping their thighs, accompanied her plaints with shrill cries.

Night was falling. An oil lamp was lit. Its flame, kindled with blood, smoked constantly. The long narrow room was drowned in a dusk light filled with the silent movements of shadows. Against the back wall, sitting huddled over on herself, my wife had another row of women standing motionless by her side. Her face was lost in the folds of a piece of snow-white gauze, such that her eyes were hidden.

From time to time a sob would burst forth, or a long drawn out wail, swollen with sighs, could be heard.

In that unfurnished, bare-walled room, nothing but the white splashes of the mourning gauze that the women had wound about their heads stood out in the dimness. At times, the faint shuffling sound of their bare feet moving around came to the ear.

At nightfall, they left the room. They all gathered in another bedroom of the house in order to have something to eat and to get some sleep. The abandoned room was plunged in obscurity; though it was already dark, night had not yet fully gathered. At the other end of the house, the voices of the women rose freely. Death's presence had not been altogether forgotten, but this death was now entering into the general order of things, people were beginning to get used to it. The women were still talking about it, they talked as if it had happened years ago already. And, in fact, in the very second one dies, doesn't he join all the other dead, the very first dead?

Conversations struck up again; the women had finished eating. Who knows what kind of fond feelings hovered in their voices which made them become thoughtful toward one another and filled each of them with secret gentleness. From time to time they would sigh, feeling submerged by a profound feeling of peace, as if their need for quietude had just been completely satisfied. Why did they feel so happy? Where was that surge of plenitude within them coming from? Toward whom were they so grateful?

I went over to my desk and began to draw up a petition.

I'll be asked: But what will your petition be about?

I'll start over again: I thank the stars for having showered favors upon me. My beloved parents left me a large house. To tell the truth, lands also fell to me . . . I'll tell you the whole story that you've just heard. Except that now we are beginning to have a mutual misunderstanding about the end.

"After that beginning," you'll tell me, "we will get down to the facts."

"What do you mean? My petition is finished!"

Yet it's true, I must admit I have lost the thread of the story; that often happens. But does that mean you have to be more demanding? You've convinced me that I couldn't have written my petition, since now you're asking me what it's about. So you didn't understand, from the minute I started talking, that it began with the first words? What happened? Why did we suddenly stop understanding one another, when it seemed we were both speaking the same language?

A petition? No, no petition. Never again. Let's think of something else.

I can barely recognize myself, it's all beyond me. I'm losing self-confidence, life is abandoning me; this tide is stronger than I am, I no longer have the strength to hold it back. Has death already taken possession of me? I've never been afraid of it, but this is strange. My ancestors are calling to me. This old house is filled with more dead than a cemetery. All my forefathers are around me. My gestures mirror all their gestures. I would like to speak, but they are speaking for me. They weigh upon my soul with infinite heaviness. I am a forest of cadavers seeking resurrection.

Yet I'm alone. A light is inexorably moving toward my eyes, it is beginning to go out, goes out, eternal, gloomy. Gradually, it destroys the taste of the air, reduces this summer night to ashes. Where is my wife's black hair? Where is her fresh body? The smell of the damp fields? It has come to obliterate everything. What is this long wall of blood I've come up against now? Forgetfulness is closing doors. Ah, woe, woe! Death is burying me. Woe is revealing me to myself, I'm dying! The dearest thing in the world to me is turning away.

I am with my ancestors, with all my dead. I'm screaming, I am the pain that accuses and curses. Why are you rising up that way? Do you want to protect me? But you're crushing me! Your truth is nothing but the truth of the dead and my heart is already filled with your decomposition. Ah! Am I shivering with cold? A little while ago my blood was burning like a blazing forge.

The last door is closing; the house is like a tomb: dark, locked up, shrouded in silence. My will tenses within me, it is resentment that is sustaining me. Would that I could live one more day, live one hour. My cruelty would surpass that of all tyrants, I would be more precise than a surgeon. I would burn, stamp out false life at its source. If anything remained after that, it would be true life. I am strong, my hatred has made me strong. Give me just one more hour to live; you people who hear me, do something. I am going to fall silent forever. One more time, before my mouth closes, is filled with earth, I will cry out. Would that my words go straight to your hearts, you who spend your life eating and sleeping! Death, I'm being devoured by death.

Now I'm moving toward those who stand against life. My

heart is eaten away with bitterness. Who will save me? Death is sudden. Now it is taking me before my porous ancestors and everything is coming to a halt. It is the steady, constant light . . .

Blinded, I'm blinded! But why am I screaming, "Save me!" Why such despair? Nothing or no one can save me. I'm no longer in control of myself; my misfortune does not depend on others. Rather, it is the law, it is our established order. I am their victim. I'm leaving because I know no other law. I'm leaving . . .

The Talisman

THOUGH BIRDSONG FILLS THE AIR

"Ah! There you are at last! Everything all right at the shop?"

"As usual, Boss. How are you this morning?"

"Don't ask! My health is a subject of conversation that no longer interests me."

Ghosli, the weaver employee, begins chuckling innocently. He's just come back from going to the market for his boss, Hocine Dermak. No longer really a young man, twenty-five, twenty-six maybe, Ghosli still carries out the chores an apprentice would. Hocine Dermak smiles also.

"So, what news have you brought? Come out with it."

"Nothing spectacular. Today just as yesterday, as the song goes."

"What a clever fellow!"

Ghosli's flat cheeks armed with prickly whiskers bulge with that same ingenuous laughter, revealing his long yellow horse teeth. He goes off to the kitchen to set down the basket weighing on his arm.

When he returns to the patio relieved of his burden, Hocine Dermak says over his shoulder, "Here, have a seat. You've earned a glass of tea."

Stretched out on a large Persian carpet, his mammillated torso covered with a sheet, he motions Ghosli over to a second divan, made up of two mattresses, as is his, covered with a blue silk quilt. The worker acquiesces, slips out of his shoes before stepping onto the interlaced woven flowers. Dermak raises himself up. From a platter on a nearby stand he lifts a teapot which releases a thick stream of tea into the glasses.

Every morning the same scene recurs between the two men.

The master weaver doesn't hide his satisfaction. Leaning on one elbow, glass in hand, he gulps down little swallows of tea, casting furtive glances at Ghosli. Every time he sees the employee, he feels as if he's been reborn. He's found a companion true to his heart to get him through the interminably idle days his illness has condemned him to.

Still leaning on one elbow, glass in hand, he thinks for a minute, nods his head, and starts drinking again.

Suddenly the words are burning to come out, "Do you know what I think, Ghosli?"

The employee stops sucking in the hot tea from the rim of his glass.

"No."

"Something about life needs changing. There's no doubt people would benefit from the change."

A smile flashes across Ghosli's eyes. He's grown accustomed to these outbursts which used to throw him into a state of complete confusion.

"For life is a trap!" Dermak resumes. (He seems to have ruminated over these thoughts for a long time.) "A well-laid trap! Haven't these nearly eight years of war, which weren't really war, but God only knows what more, or what less, haven't they been a trap? And what other trap have we become ensnared in now, eh? No one can know, until the day it will be too late to get out! No, we'd be better off just throwing up the whole game!"

He observes a brief period of silence, and then adds in a sad voice, "But is that possible?"

Ghosli says to himself, "What a strange man! He's been so damned successful in life. Why does he need to torment himself like this?"

"That's what living's about," he answers.

He doesn't really have a clear idea of what he meant by those words. He thought they would calm Dermak down.

"That's what everyone believes!" protests Dermak. "My business has expanded quite a bit in the last twenty years and continues to prosper despite a turndown due to political events. I now own two shops equipped with twelve looms each. Well, this achievement, of which I can rightfully be proud, is nothing but a trap as well!"

Ghosli listens to the master weaver without saying anything more. These thoughts could not be haunting Dermak had his melancholy mood this morning not stubbornly fed upon them.

The arcades with their blue limewashed pillars embracing the patio attenuate the harsh light of day. The overflow from the pool, partly hidden by a bed of four-o'clocks and basil, drains out in a steady trickle. Reflections of cool water are constantly glimmering about the courtyard. The stillness creeps over Ghosli. He sinks into thought, but encounters only the infinite sensation of the summer morning surrounding him.

"Do you understand that?" Hocine Dermak asks.

Ghosli comes out of his daydream, lets out a sigh.

Somewhat confusedly, he answers, "I understand, but I don't agree with you."

"You don't say! And why not? Would you mind explaining?"

Ghosli looks at him, surprised.

"I have other ideas."

"Other ideas! What ideas? Let's hear them. That's a good one for you. Other ideas!"

Caught off guard, the employee starts thinking. Annoyed by his silence, the master weaver shouts, "Say something! Let's discuss it! Why have you stopped talking?

Ghosli agrees reluctantly.

"I don't know how to discuss things. In my opinion discussions only aggravate misunderstandings."

"So in your opinion there can only be misunderstandings between people?"

"No, maybe not. I have no idea, to be truthful."

"So what exactly did you mean to say?"

"That it is stupid to have a discussion to find out the truth."

Taken aback, Hocine Dermak cannot find the words to answer him and breaks out in annoyed laughter. Ghosli smiles at his boss with a conniving look.

The master weaver grabs a teaspoon and begins to tap on the tray with it. An unpleasant sensation of irritation is rising within him and making him tremble.

The clinking sound draws Tetma to the doorway of one of the rooms. The appearance of the woman, whose handsome features—and most of all those huge grey eyes set off from the rest of her face with a line of kohl—always surprise Ghosli, gives Hocine Dermak's exasperation an excuse to explode.

"No one called you! What's come over you, wanting to stick your nose into something that's none of your business?"

"I thought you needed something."

Having calmly uttered those words, she turns and walks away.

Dermak grumbles, "You're naïve. You've gotten it into your head that everyone knows where the truth lies, that the first imbecile who comes along can see it. You're mistaken. If you want to live according to the truth, begin by taking off your jacket, your shoes, walk around in a loincloth! And thus in your nudity, with head bowed, go before your Creator! Then you will see what men say about you."

His round face squinches up. This irritated outburst has worn him out. He stretches himself, drops his head down into the pillows. He feels so much pity for himself and for everything else, he has a lump in his throat.

Eyes closed, he resumes.

"Man, being the idiot he is, will continue to suffer, though birdsong fills the air."

Opening his eyes the next instant, he says, "Don't resent me for what I just said."

He remains lying down, eyes turned toward the worker.

"How many are capable of knowing where the truth lies?" he asks with a deep sigh. "Ah, living is so difficult . . ."

Suddenly he raises himself up and leans back on his elbow again.

"Don't listen to the preachers! It will mean your downfall. You are still young, you haven't done enough fighting yet, and you haven't grown hard-hearted. Don't expect life to treat you and the others any less unjustly today!"

He glares darkly at God knows what, then lies back down. This time, as if there were nothing more to be said, he falls into an abysmal silence.

The master weaver's face relaxes, an alert serenity descends upon it. Ghosli does not interrupt this meditation.

Hocine Dermak nevertheless comes out of his silence to ask in a distant voice, "Would you like to have lunch with us?"

"I'd love to."

Still lying down, his gaze lost in the heavens, Dermak calls out in an ordinary voice, "Tetma! Tetma!"

Looking equally imperturbable, the woman reappears. Ghosli is again fascinated by her. No matter how hard he tries, he cannot imagine her being a brothel keeper as rumor has it.

"Ghosli's staying for lunch."

"That's very nice of him," she approves.

As she turns toward the worker, her dark, almost alarming eyes lose their grief-stricken expression and fill with a bright smile.

She walks away, leaving the two men alone together.

The sound of the water running out of the pool begins trickling between them again. That same feeling of peacefulness floods over Ghosli, each instant melts into all the others, taking on the weight of eternity, so that time ultimately—as if it had been absorbed—withdraws from the world. Only the silent presence of this summer morning is left lingering between things.

Suddenly, in a clump of twittering rumpled feathers, two sparrows come swooping into the courtyard, resolved to settle their quarrel there.

Hocine Dermak raises himself up to observe them and lets out a long delighted laugh.

"Ah, the little rascals, just look at the way they're bickering! Isn't that incredible?"

Frightened by the voice, the birds soar quickly away, still pursuing one another, and disappear over the terrace.

Hocine Dermak lies down on his left side, smiles and grumbles with a tired look on his face, "Hoard, save—and toil for this? How completely idiotic!"

He cranes his neck out toward Ghosli.

"Live by your instincts."

The employee assents with a nod of the head.

Exhausted, the master weaver changes positions again; he lies down flat on his back and pulls the pillows that have slipped over to one side back under his head. He breathes in a deep lungful of air, lets it out. As a result, his bloated body, which seemed to encumber him before, relaxes. He feels as if—and Ghosli senses it too—he is becoming detached from things and withdrawing into a cave filled with shadows.

He murmurs to himself, "Peace."

Ghosli feels his heart sink slightly, but comforting words come rapidly to his mind.

"I am not the one whom death is awaiting."

He listens to the pool babbling and returns to the enchanting summer morning.

"So?" asks Hocine Dermak, as if in a dream. "In your opinion, people intend to loot us, or am I mistaken?"

That voice which had suddenly turned mocking again!

"Goods and property must be shared out equally," responds Ghosli hesitantly.

"So you think that . . ."

"Thousands of people think the same thing."

"It's true, no one is happy."

Hocine Dermak remains quiet for a long moment.

"No!" he declares categorically all of a sudden. "People are not discontent for the reason you think. No, my friend, there's another reason! A completely different reason! I can sense it. I'm not sure what, but it's something else. I—I am—sure of it!"

He falls silent again, but is obviously still thinking. His eyes gaze out blankly. His cheeks are sunken from his eyes all the way down to the corners of his mouth.

Nevertheless, the coolness and the diffuse light in which the patio is bathed envelop Ghosli's heart in a halo of incorruptible well-being.

"The Hocine Dermaks of the world will just have to up and disappear. That's the only thing left for them to do, when it comes right down to it," he says to himself. "Yes! That's the only thing left for them to do."

Beside him, as if having been relieved of a burden, the master weaver is breathing more regularly. He seems to be slipping off into a light sleep.

Yet shortly afterward, he confides in a slow, steady voice, articulating each word clearly, "I feel as if I'm dying."

He stares at Ghosli.

"We die a little every day, but what I just experienced, what we call experiencing . . . It's strange! It was like a burning feeling."

He sinks back into thought, or is overwhelmed with drowsiness; one can't tell.

"What's strange?" Ghosli asks himself. "Dying? Being aware of it?"

He heaves a sigh, his spirit—now freer and easier—takes possession of the large house, with its pool and its flowers. The endless reflections of the water shimmering around the courtyard. What delightful calm!

Tetma's black eyes are watching Hocine Dermak. They darken even more, and then with a mournful glimmer remain still. After having, with uncertain steps, wandered interminably from one corner to the other of the night-filled patio, Dermak headed toward the main door of the house, opened it, stepped through . . .

Engulfed immediately in the dark mist—a fuliginous cloud studded with pinpoints of light—he staggers. He wants to turn back, but it—swooping down upon him—thumps him on the back; blinds him. It pushes him onward. He keeps going. Allows himself to be swept along.

"How many months has it been since I've been out of doors?"

The cloud roils within him, he's not sure anymore; after all, he doesn't look all that different from the people standing watch whom he passes from time to time along his way. He's shod simply with a pair of indoor slippers, on his shoulders he wears a gabardine thrown over his gandoura, but they aren't any more dressed than he is. He drifts through the darkness.

He dreams, gazes deeply into his own eyes, sees the city of shadows—in the throes of a reptatorial movement—bump up against the edges of the night. A dry heat makes him begin to pant. He feels the corners of a can becoming encrusted in the palm of his hand; he hears conversations, whisperings. And he wanders about. Wanders about among the traffic lights, the obstacles of a haphazard town.

Nevertheless, the ever-present obstacles slip aside and open up a passageway for him out to the other end which is beckoning to him. A low heavy door set in a long wall. Which suddenly materializes before him. He searches the pockets of his overcoat. He is holding the key. He opens the door. A breath, or rather a clammy hand presses up against his face. Thicker and more acrid than all those which melt together within it, and the smell of suint which revives him afterward! He breathes it in. He forgets his long years of illness, of boredom, of dreariness.

He makes his way down toward the opaque depths. One foot is set carefully down beside the other on each step before going on to the next. Having reached the bottom of the stairway, he walks on blindly. The rancid, moldy smells seem to emanate from the shadows gathered there. He can feel shades looming all around him. "They're there, they can feel my presence." He reaches out with his free arm and touches a beam. He strokes the sheets of tight warp threads, which vibrate like a fascicle of nerves. Then his palm falls upon a spool. He turns it with one finger. The spool answers with a deep and gentle purring sound. The other looms and the warper are waiting as well. All things that recognize him, that have remained faithful to him.

Then he opens the can he's holding in his hand and pours out its contents. Immediately a cold, volatile smell disperses the old odors. Dermak strikes a match, making a phosphorescent streak. Two, three, then four flashes follow. Nothing happens. He grows impatient, strikes more matches. A small fire blooms suddenly down close to the floor, a few others come to life a little farther away and begin to dance. How quickly they multiply, leap about, blaze high! Imitating one another, they light up the cellar just for him.

He turns his back on them, walks over to the staircase,

climbs the narrow steps, locks the door. On his way back, he again takes streets he barely recognizes.

He finds Tetma still sitting in the same place.

She stands up when she sees him. She takes him over to his bed, murmuring, "Lie down. Rest."

Dermak motions her away. She takes off his gabardine and leaves the room. He rests his head on the pillows, lies down on his right side, and heaves a sigh.

LA CUADRA

A chaos of sheet metal, crates, flattened oil drums, old boards . . . The only stone building standing there was engulfed in the shanties, they seemed to be attacking it, driving it back. The horde of them, built leaning up against the surrounding wall, was a dark seething mass even when there was no one about. However, the stables, known as *la cuadra,* almost never remained empty, even for an instant. A swarm of kids were constantly cavorting there, letting out shrill cries, some perched upon the heaps of garbage and manure piled up in all corners, others on stacks of wood, mounds of rubble, piles of rusted scrap metal. They were all dirty, unkempt, in rags; they ran after one another, thrashed each other, rolled around in the dust together.

That morning, a handful of them were hanging around the well. They were standing in the fetid mud at its edge; suddenly, in a mad dash and an explosion of shouts, they scattered. Two little girls remained leaning over the well, their bottoms showing from under their tattered dresses. They contemplated the glassy surface sleeping under the earth. They were trying to see their reflections, taking turns spitting and waiting. The muffled plop came echoing up between the walls, the surface of the water began to ripple, they watched it in silence, spit again.

The others had discovered a dying cat on some detritus that had not yet finished rotting. Eyes gouged out, fur falling off in clumps, the animal wasn't moving. Emboldened, a wrinkled little urchin tied a string on the end of its tail and ran off as fast as he could, dragging the cat behind him. The troop followed him, shrieking with joy. The cat began to bound about. The kids were at the height of excitement. Some of them picked up rocks and took potshots at it. The cat was howling ferociously, making tremendous leaps that threw it every which way. Then the boy pulling it took off at a dead run, his eyes rolled back in his head.

A shower of stones rained quickly down upon the cat. Gathered in a circle around it, the children observed its crushed, bloody cadaver. Just for an instant, then took off running again.

While the dead animal, still tied to the string, stirred up the dust in the camp, they continued to bombard it with all sorts of projectiles.

At the well, the two little girls leaning on their elbows at its edge had stopped spitting and were talking.

"Your mother won't ever come back, Pamela."

"Yes, she will come back!"

"You haven't the slightest idea. Why do you say she'll come back?"

"Because."

"Maybe the man she left with won't let her come back."

"She'll come back, I tell you."

"Well I'm telling you he won't let her."

"I know she'll come back."

"Why doesn't your father go and get her?"

"My dad won't budge. He's waiting. He's always asking me to go and get him a bottle of wine. And he's just waiting. She'll come back of her own accord."

"And what if she doesn't?"

Pamela remained silent.

"If she's not here on Sunday, I'll let myself fall into this well."

Together they look at the water and its cold sheen lying in wait deep below.

"Is that true? Would you be able to do that? No, you liar!"

"Just wait and see if I'm lying, Carmelita."

Barefoot, with her ample shape stuffed into a black dress, all shiny with wear, a portly woman came out of a shack, an infant hanging at her breast. She planted herself in front of the doorway, noticed the two little girls. The woman immediately began to shout as loud as she could, "Carmelita! Carmelita! Come here!"

Carmelita abandoned her companion, pranced hurriedly away, and saw that her mother was glaring at Pamela standing alone near the well. Then she saw her spit in disgust.

"Dirty scum! A slut's daughter."

"What's a slut, mama?" asked Carmelita lifting her grimy face toward her mother.

"A slut? Here's what it is!"

With her free hand Rosa smacked the girl's outstretched mug. Carmelita doubled over sobbing.

Ripping the suckling child from her breast, the gypsy shoved it into her daughter's arms. The little girl staggered under the weight and licked her salty tears. Arching her back, sniffling, she got a grip on Joselito as best she could. Her mother gave her a stern look and, for a finishing touch, threatened her with her fist while eyeing the other girl, before going back into the shack.

In the distance the other kids, having found a new game, were running and shouting gaily at the top of their lungs through the cuadra.

Romeo—four years old at the most—stood leaning against the hull of a Dodge, scratching at the yellow paint on one of its doors with his fingernail. A stained tunic hung down to the middle of his thighs. His little face was shiny with snot. He was happy, no question about that. Carmelita walked up to him. He didn't deign to look at her, but his face darkened, lost its happy look. He went around to the other side of the truck.

Carmelita sat down on the ground, leaning her back against the front wheel. She sat her brother down between her outstretched legs and busied herself tidying the curls that were falling into his eyes. The little imp took the opportunity to scramble away on his hands and knees.

"Joselito! Joselito!"

She caught up with him and began cuddling him, making him walk on his feet while she held his little fists.

Mama Rosa reappeared. Salah was walking past.

"Is it already noon, Salah?" she exclaimed. "*Carajo!* Damn it! I haven't done a thing yet!"

Joselito crawled over to her, clung to her ankles. Carmelita wanted to take him back. The gypsy woman lifted him up with one hand and sat him astride her hip. She remained standing in the same place, her eyes gazing out into the distance. Joselito twisted around, shoved his distended belly into his mothers side. But dazed, she didn't move. He screamed out in rage. With a distracted gesture, Rosa stuffed her breast into his mouth. The brat calmed down.

The gypsy woman went back into her shack with him. Drawn aside for an instant, the sackcloth covering the entrance showed a glint of metal pots.

The tinsmith and the cooper closed up shop. They were on their way home. Their shacks were adjacent to one another. The former, a stocky Spaniard dressed in overalls that hugged his legs and torso, was pushing a bicycle.

He was saying, "No, my wife wouldn't be able to make flat bread."

The other, a scrawny, bearded Algerian wearing traditional garb—loose-fitting pants and a short vest—kept repeating, "Do as we do, it won't cost you much. Homemade bread costs less and is more nourishing."

"My wife would never be able to make flat bread!"

"If you send her over to my house, we'll teach her how."

They walked on a little further together. Then the tinsmith said, "I'd better get going, Ba Ahmed. Good-bye."

"Good-bye, Juanico. Send her over: we'll show her how!"

The Spaniard mounted his old bike and, peddling hard, steered toward the gate of the cuadra.

"Adios!" he called, with a big wave of his arm.

A flawless summer night surrounds the shacks. The blind man scatters the notes of his guitar out in little flourishes. From time to time, as if in spite of himself, his voice bursts forth as well. Perched up very high, yelping, it lets out words that are something other than words: a fierce recrimination.

Salah was floundering in the swamp of sleep. He murmured

a silent order, "Choose the block of stone that is least heavy to carry and come back slowly. Use up time. Choose a stone, the best one . . ." The voice of the blind man awakens him. He recognizes his shack. He's been dreaming about the camp where he was detained again. He drifts off once more to explore a watchful reality, looming beyond tangible things. Making his way across the cuadra, he is surprised at being able to get away without finding internment camps everywhere clamped down over human prey. The wailing of the blind man accompanies him in his wandering. Having been turned away, Salah comes straight back and is washed up on this bank again, he feels as if something has closed up behind him. He turns around, sees nothing. He moves forward, finds only that voice.

Three years earlier, he'd wandered in like that too, and heard the same chanting. Maria, the wife of the blind man, had just died. To do so, she'd simply given a thump with the palm of her hand: she was trying to drive a cork into the neck of a bottle. But the needle she'd stuck in the cork broke off in her hand. First they amputated one hand. After that, they never stopped cutting that woman up.

Salah had learned her story, and many others, as soon as he'd settled in the cuadra.

The blind man's voice fell silent again.

"What do you want? Why are you just standing there like that? Why are you looking at me that way?" scolded the young girl. "Can't you think of anything better to do? Why don't you go get some air someplace else? What do you want!" Paca shouted again. "If you're expecting something from me, you'll be a long time waiting . . ."

"I hate to bother you, dear," interrupted Rafael, "but could you tell me who was here a few minutes ago?"

He was only two steps away. He was pulling back the branches of a young fig tree whose roots had taken hold in the surrounding wall. Then he let them snap into the leaves like the lash of a whip: blinding dust sifted down all around, covering everything.

"Can you tell me the guy's name? There was someone here

a few minutes ago. What was he doing here? You can't tell me there was no one here."

Turning around, Paca made ready to leave. But first she declared, "I don't know what you're talking about."

The look she gave him through the wisps of hair hanging about her face made something in Rafael falter.

A mask with empty eye sockets began cursing at her. Paca didn't raise an eyebrow.

Rafael stopped. He said in a low voice, "I saw you together yesterday too. You can't deny it, I saw you. People looked at me funny when I walked by this morning."

The silence that had crept between them filled with the wild cries of the youngsters and the heaving of the cuadra panting like an exhausted beast.

"You'd better not . . . ," began Paca.

A dry click: the blade of a knife snapped into Rafael's hand.

The young girl's eyes dilated with fear. Clenching her teeth, she held back a scream.

The knife disappeared.

"Just keep messing around like this," said Rafael. "Just keep it up, you'll see what will happen."

She remained petrified.

"Go on. Get out of here."

The man let out a cracked laugh.

A moment of hesitation and, knees wobbling, Paca walked away.

She immediately whirled around. With a sharp whistle, the knife had just stuck into the wall of a shack behind her. The blade was still quivering.

The girl's lips twisted into a grimace of hatred. Rafael laughed.

Paca walked off, throwing her hair back onto her shoulders. Once again, every movement of her body expressed animal defiance.

The morning was wearing on. With his bad eyes, from deep within his lair old man Blanès watched the sunlight spreading, devouring the cuadra, and cursed. Using a broom, he went on stirring the grilled chickpeas, known as *torraïcos,* over a glowing brazier. He was swearing enough to bring the heavens crashing down: they would never be ready for this afternoon! Miss a Sunday sale; how stupid could you get! Naked down to the waist, he rocked his thick torso, powdered with ashes, harder.

Meanwhile, creeping stealthily in, young scamps came to steal whole fistfuls from the open sack beside him. With the broom, he lashed out blindly at them, but rarely hit his mark. Someone was prowling around in front of the door. Blanès could barely make out the silhouette that was passing back and forth like a shadow, but he wasn't in the least worried, he recognized it: it was old Zohra. She went digging around in all the piles of garbage and sometimes succeeded in pulling out some unidentifiable object from one of them. She would scrutinize the find for a long while; then toss it away with a shrug. Then she would start prowling around again. Her lips were moving too, as usual. A pack of children burst noisily out of old man Blanès's shack and almost knocked her over. They gave her such a fright she went to sit down in a corner.

She watched all those riotous little devils with a glazed expression. Without even thinking about it, she murmured, "Blessed are they, blessed!"

Suddenly, tears were rolling down her wilted cheeks.

As it had begun to grow hotter, feeling as if she were smothering, she rose to her feet. Zohra made her way across the courtyard that had turned into a vat of molten lead. With the exception of the kids, all the inhabitants had taken shelter.

Consuelo, Eduardo's wife, and her daughter Josefa appeared in the midst of the blazing heat. They had both just gotten back from town. Faces flushed and streaming with sweat, each carried a wicker basket on her arm overflowing with multicolored ribbons and rolls of lace, with which they had made the rounds of the Moorish quarters.

They passed the old woman. Consuelo said loudly, "*Ay ay, qué calor, Mama Zohra!* What heat!"

"Yes, child."

Without stopping, wiping her forehead with a handkerchief, "You shouldn't stay outside, Mama Zohra!"

"Yes, child."

From the cooper's cabin rose the persistent dull pounding of a wooden mallet. Just then Francisco suddenly appeared from a stable between two snorting mares he was holding tightly by their bridles. He quickly reached the gate with them and disappeared. As a sideline to his job as a sheep shearer or dog clipper, Francisco occasionally worked as a healer; therefore people often brought him sick animals.

Consuelo and Josefa had hurried back home. The kids came galloping past again. Old Zohra considered them with two dry eyes this time. She wasn't thinking of anything anymore. As if they were whirling about in some other universe, suddenly their voices and their noisy stampeding reached her ears seemingly purified and free of violence.

She walked over toward a sort of niche.

"I'm tired, my children, so very tired!" she muttered crouching down to take shelter there.

Standing stiffly in front of his door, Rico had been bellowing in a groggy voice for several minutes.

"Pamela! . . . Pamela!"

A beard of several days covered his face in which his watery eyes floated. No one answered him, or even seemed to hear his calls. He went on, glumly persistent, "Pamela! . . . Pamela! . . . Bitch!"

Suddenly, the children, imitating his hoarse voice, yelled out in chorus, "Pamela! . . . Pamela! . . . Bitch!"

He answered them with obscenities and attempted to run after them. But he took only one step, staggered, and nearly fell flat on the ground.

The children shouted all the louder.

"*Borracho! Dido borracho!* Drunkard!"

Legs spread, teetering, the man hurled invectives at them with all the strength he could muster.

Drawn by the hubbub, people came out of their shacks. Rico

went into his, mumbling curses at them all. The kids grew even more excited. They went closer and obstinately began chanting again.

"Pamela, Pamela . . . *Dido borracho!*"

"Gotta find that mule-headed girl! Get a move on! Come on!" a woman bawled. "Maybe her father needs her."

Other curious faces showed themselves.

"Where did she go?"

The muttering swelled, a nervous tension fell over the sun-baked cuadra. The band of urchins, accompanied by some adults, had gone off in search of the little girl. People were calling to her from all sides, her name was echoing from one end of the camp to the other. The neighbors who didn't feel like getting involved stood watching it all from their doorsteps. Unkind words were flying about. Young Carmelita had not joined the search either. She walked nonchalantly around the well, cast a furtive glance into it and made her way back.

Pamela's name was still being called in the distance. The children and the adults, caught up in the search, had begun shouting.

A half an hour went by; Pamela was still not to be found.

From that moment on, Carmelita sat in the shade of the shacks and her eyes, gleaming with a sort of feverish triumph, remained riveted on the well.

Mama Rosa pointed to her from afar; then pointed to the infant clinging to her skirt.

"What a pity! What have we done to warrant God sending us this calamity?"

She glared up at the sky, frowning.

Just then a raucous clamor arose, followed by a row. The children were scuffling around in front of old man Blanès's place over something they were fiercely tearing out of each other's hands. The old man's broom emerged from the heap of bodies. Blanès used innumerable brooms for stirring his chick-peas. Then when they were worn out, he would toss them to the children, who tore them to shreds and were able to pick out a good number of torraïcos from them!

When there was nothing left of the broom but debris, the search began again.

Not a trace of Pamela anywhere!

People grew weary of searching. The kids went back to their cavorting, the adults returned to their shacks grumbling.

The last one, the girl Josefa, was making her way around Mama Zohra's hovel when the sound of crying caught her attention. It sounded sort of like a song being hummed and was so faint that she thought it was an illusion at first. She decided to stick her head in between the ill-joined planks. Pamela was inside! Squatting in front of Mama Zohra, it was she who was sobbing. The little old lady, seated as well, was holding her hand, frozen-faced. She was gazing at her with what seemed to be a smile but at the same time her eyes were filled with a terrifying emptiness. A cold shudder ran up Josefa's spine. She suddenly understood: Zohra was dead.

She pounced on Pamela, tore her from where she sat. The old woman didn't move; only her arm fell stiffly to the floor.

Josefa ran out, clutching the child to her breast, letting out a heart-wrenching moan.

Everyone in the cuadra came out this time.

"Did they find her? What's wrong with her?"

"She was at Mama Zohra's," Josefa said in a gasp, her throat dry. "She's dead."

Salah patted the little girl's hands.

"Dead! You've gone soft in the head! Just look at her! There's nothing wrong with her! Look at her!"

"No, the old woman," said Josefa with her voice still quavering. "*La vieja!* The old woman!"

"Oh! Oh! *Madre mía!*"

The gypsies signed themselves.

Carmelita pushed her way forward, elbowed up to the front of the crowd of onlookers. She drew near Pamela, who was still sobbing softly. Reaching out her hand, she touched her. She looked at Pamela for a few minutes, then beat a retreat.

A second later she was rolling around on the ground, frothing at the mouth.

"No! No! It isn't true!"

Mama Rosa grabbed her by the arm and shook her. Far from calming down, the girl attempted to pull her mother down to the ground. The gypsy woman saw red. She struck out at her vigorously before anyone could intervene. But the child fought back so furiously that she got away and the gypsy woman burst out cursing her.

"Have you been possessed or something? Ay, you demon! You're inhabited by the devil! Bad seed, it's the devil!"

Men and women came between them to protect the little girl. Then the mother, brandishing her fists, roared, "She's my daughter! Let me have her! So what if I want to kill her? If I want to beat her to a pulp? Who s going to stop me? *La puta!* The slut!"

She managed to drag the girl away. From the shack rose shrieks as if someone were being skinned alive.

"No! No! It isn't true!"

Each of Carmelita's shouts were answered by her mother's blows and her barking voice.

"Pest! You've been cursed! It's the devil! The devil!"

THE STONE INSCRIPTION

That slab of stone set into the wall, I'm walking past it again! A burial stone no doubt. One of those very commonplace burial stones that once stood guard at the head if not at the foot of someone's remains, and whose sheer numbers leave people who visit our cemeteries with such an odd impression. The impression of an exodus, I'd say, yes—as paradoxical as that may sound—and a taciturn, obstinate exodus at that. Much less than any others should these burial stones be leaving the fields of repose where, each engraved with the family name of the underground inhabitant over whose sleep they keep watch, the age-old ritual brings them together. Yet nothing can be done about it, those deserters go ahead and leave. They leave for their destinations, known only to themselves, taking with them the names and the last traces of the departed who were entrusted to them. One would swear they disappeared to answer a call, to fulfill their destiny.

And the orphaned souls, does anyone think about what becomes of them? Forlorn, they've surely been abandoned to even deeper shadows, to a more voracious consumption.

And so one runs into these steles all over the place. Mixed in with unsophisticated stones come straight from their quarries, they're used for paving streets, the courtyards of houses, canals, pools, stairways. But rarely are they used for building the wall of an enclosure or a house like the one I have the privilege of contemplating here. And even more rarely, if ever, are their inscriptions turned outward, for all to see. Yes, customarily their legible sides are buried. Why? . . . Probably in an attempt to bring new innocence to these renegades. Granted, with not a single mark to draw the eye, they are as good as dead, at least in their own way. Had those nitwits seen it coming? Had they known before deserting the gardens of peace and throwing themselves into the hands of humans that they would be condemned to this fate? That they would be gradually annihilated? And that the text they bore would be destroyed along with them?

It is hope that drives them, the presentiment that a privileged few will survive. There is no doubt about that. If not, how could that roving temperament, that penchant for nomadism be explained? And this is without dispute the case when it comes to the stone before me, which seems to be bearing witness for them all, establishing the rationality of the bizarre migration.

But survive, be saved in what way? In my opinion, in a way that would ensure the transmission of a message they were all entrusted with. For I am absolutely certain that these stones bear a message. Therefore it would suffice for only one of them to escape while the others went to increase the stock of everyday construction materials!

In this case, the desire to renew their candor and innocence by immuring their inscriptions would seem neither candid nor innocent on the part of human beings: rather, it would reveal a deliberate and carefully devised plan of destruction.

"But of what?" you will ask. "Destruction of what? Aren't the stones used twice rather than once, and even in a more useful way the second time?"

That is where the uncertainty begins, where hypotheses can only be put forth with caution.

I have been of this opinion ever since a recent change of residence placed this stone inscription on my path approximately at eye level. Not a day goes by without the sight of it intriguing, disturbing, and puzzling me.

This morning, having already gone three steps past it, suddenly I turn around. My about-face is accompanied by a sort of annoyed gesture. I immediately laugh about it and draw nearer to the object of my curiosity. I examine it attentively. A page from a large book of sandstone by the looks of it. An absolutely ordinary object, all things considered. Mold spreads verdigris over its surface—covered, peopled, seething with engraved signs. The tablet is fitted into a wall that is the only one of its kind in our town: it runs continuously along the whole length of the street, turning when the street turns, and ends up encircling a whole neighborhood! The materials—rubble, bricks, blocks of gray stone of varying sizes, shingles, dirt, sand, even pebbles—it is made up of also constitute a unique work of masonry owing to the incongruous and disorderly mixture. Another particularity of the wall, its great age—as could be proven, if necessary, by the negligence of its construction—but from what period is it exactly? I wouldn't even attempt an approximate guess, given my ignorance of history, which has never really interested me—apparently the only thing that keeps it standing is its breadth, the precise measure of which is unknown but one can imagine it being huge. Oh, it will remain standing for a long time yet, I'm certain of that! One last distinctive thing, the materials were left bare, as my description has shown you, bare, contrary to the custom everywhere else of covering them with plaster. As far back as I can remember, the inhabitants have always deplored it as a monstrosity unworthy of our town. And in fact, no word would be strong enough to express the feeling of offence and annoyance that fills us at the sight of such negligence. Nevertheless, there's not a soul to be found who would suggest or even think that the problem should be remedied.

As for myself, the wall has also led me to hold my ancestors' industry, their skill, their builders' ardor in low esteem. What's more, this deficiency doesn't surprise me in the least. I have always suspected them of professing, if not disdain, at least indifference for things of bricks and mortar. Which doesn't cause me to disapprove, if you follow me, but rather to approve of them. I, who look with equal indifference upon the vain pride of architects, and entrepreneurs, their vulgar fondness for those piles of stones they call: edifices, palaces, monuments! A good deal can be said about the subject.

And first about the embarrassment that this wall, which does not conceal its nudity, arouses in my fellow citizens. But are the other walls, smooth and plastered as they may be, of any better quality? I'd bet a thousand to one that, upon closer examination, they would prove to be made up various and sundry items as well, and that the only difference to be found would be in the care that had been taken to cover up the hodgepodge!

Therefore, of what use is it to express hypocritical indignation if ultimately things everywhere are equally mediocre? Why give oneself the illusion of insisting upon an excellence that no one has ever truly felt the need for?

But, for the time being, it is not my aim to address these questions.

Though it means losing a few minutes, I have determined to decrypt the signs that are on the front of the stele. Let's begin. This time when I leave here, my curiosity must be satisfied. At first glance, I read, or believe I have read, the beginning of a verse: "*We offered to confide our secrets* . . ." I go on from memory: "*. . . to the heavens, the earth, and the mountains. All refused to accept them, all trembled at the notion of receiving them. But man agreed to take them on. He is violent and reckless.*" Carved into a gravestone, these words don't seem unusual to me. Just as I am about to walk away, however, I look more closely at the characters before my eyes. They've become jumbled! I can no longer recognize the words my lips have just pronounced! An incomprehensible mix-up has caused me to make up those sentences, which don't appear on the slab of stone at all! When you come to think of it, it's a frequent error, due to the impatience that often makes our inner consciousness get ahead of our intellect in comprehending things. It provides us with facts that, because our memory is always quick to back them up, are all the more fortuitous, as if to amuse itself at our expense!

I draw nearer to the tablet, attempt to read the text that is truly inscribed there. Pronounced wear and the decrepit state of the stone, along with the damage done by lichens, immediately complicate the task. And I find the difficulty, which arises when I was least expecting it, refreshing. "No matter!" I say to myself. "Just a little more patience and it will all become clear."

I soon recognize the familiar aspect of a few words. But . . . Impossible! The characters are too spaced out, too far apart to follow one another coherently and make it possible for me to piece some terms back together. Fine. They'll provide me with reference points, which are always useful in this type of undertaking. Forewarned and a bit wary thanks to these initial disappointments, I'll not move on and start on the second word until I've become certain of the first. Little by little I'll eliminate any risk of error. But the first word itself turns out to be half-erased; just imagine how legible the others must be. So I move back up to the first letter and put it to the test of intense scrutiny. Suddenly, the written form its neighbors take on becomes uncertain, fanciful, lending itself to several interpretations that are so different they seem contradictory! Before my very eyes, false terms form and proliferate in that conglomerate of letters and signs that erosion has chopped up and isolated arbitrarily, within real words this time, but faded, blurry.

I am obliged to admit that I have failed in my task. I step back, then start over. All the characters slip through my fingers again like sand! It's gone beyond the limits of my feeble powers of concentration. It is as if the slab of stone has soaked up all meaning and gone back to the absolute concreteness of its stone state. I am running up against a solid brick wall. I try to find a solution. While I was trying to understand the hieroglyph . . . what happened? Did I enter a labyrinth and get shut up inside without realizing it? I have to find the way out! I'm not going to panic over so little. I'm under the very distinct impression that I'm not far from my kind, despite feeling smothered, despite the web of lines that are tightening around me and holding me prisoner. With a strong push, I'll manage to get free.

I've gotten involved in an adventure that could cost me dearly, I'm willing to admit that. But where did this urge to read a chance inscription, encountered in passing, come from and why? What prompted me to do it? My destiny? Come now! What has been lost? Me? You must be joking! Will these evasive words, having drifted up from God knows where, which take pleasure in appearing to be the infallible witnesses of everything that has ever been and, probably, ever will be, condemn me to being eternally interred because I did not know how to decipher them? If I wasn't able to, it's because they eluded all my attempts and are still fleeing now! Why are they hiding behind a screen, pretending to be worn? I would like nothing better than to read them, but there are limits! How has my conduct justified such severity, what have I done to merit such torment?

Perhaps I am nothing but an offering through which our world hoped to win over some unknown thing. Yes, perhaps I'm just a victim given up in sacrifice. That's the reason, the only reason, that all communication between human beings and me has suddenly ceased! And it all began the moment I stopped in front of that inscription. I was torn from the world at that very instant. And now I am being submerged on every side, sucked into the abyss.

O bottomless abyss of meaning: one word, would that I could spell but one word! It would encompass all the others and bring them all back to life! Then I would be saved!

But I am seized with terror at the thought of . . .

No, I don't want to sink into that madness; I'm going to discover the first word. *The first!*

THE DESTINATION

The flaps of a dark-colored cloak whipped against his knees in the mountain wind as he stood silently waiting amid the pines and cypresses. He remained waiting even after Chadly appeared. From under the dusty tagelmust wrapped about his head, the razor-sharp gleam of his eyes blazed out, retreated. He was holding on a leash a dog whose coat was the color of earth. The beast was growling.

"Quiet!" he ordered the dog gruffly.

Chadly was still moving toward him. The dog suddenly grew furious, lunging on his leash. It would have torn him to shreds.

"Quiet!" the man repeated.

He jerked the animal to make it stop.

From a distance, Chadly asked, "Are we leaving?"

The other didn't answer. He walked away. Chadly followed and was soon walking beside him. The wide, rutted red dirt path, strewn with stones, with branches, tunneled deep into the woods. Chadly was on the man's left; the beast, still irascible, was on his right. They made as little noise as shadows.

An odor of ether and resin sifted down from the pines, which from time to time swelled up in a whispering backwash. The stiff trunks stood in close formation on all sides.

They climbed the flank of the eminence, reached the top.

The edge of a cliff stopped them. Chadly glanced down at the bottom of the precipice. The granite wall fell in a sheer drop into the equally dense forest clinging to its sides.

Without a word, the man began walking along the crest; the dog went out ahead. Chadly stepped out, as they had, onto the narrow ledge of rock. As he moved forward, he drew gradually closer to the precipice. Several times, his foot almost slipped, and just as many times sweat drenched his body. His movements were framed against a blurry background; he took each step as determinedly as a sleepwalker.

He reached a crevice in the rock; he had no strength left, his legs were shaking.

The man was stopped there, kneeling, and was tying a cord around the dog's chest. Chadly watched him, his head buzzing. The animal then docilely allowed itself to be lowered into the hole.

As long as the descent lasted, it kept still.

The lasso went limp; the man let it slip from his hands. He gripped the rocks jutting out from the cliff wall.

"Our turn," he called.

With surprising agility, he too disappeared into the well-like cavity.

Chadly went in next. It was easier for him to make it to the bottom, using the handholds, than it had been to face the precipice a few minutes earlier.

The three of them met up at the foot of the cliff. Chadly looked at the man, then at the mass of granite. It seemed even more forbidding than it had at the top. His companion didn't even seem to notice it.

Without resting, they started down the other side.

The forest came to an end. At its edge were rows of vineyards.

The group continued out in the open along a narrow white dusty road with two parallel ruts. They walked past the last clumps of pines and reached the plain.

The fields stretched all the way out to the horizon, fringed with a chain of mountains. Deserted. One would have thought that an invisible border had just been crossed. The sea of frothy vineyards with copper reflections came rushing up to meet them. The sky had grown alert. An airy evening sky, filled with light.

Chadly was surprised at what he felt. It was the first day he'd spent out of doors in eight months. He sucked in the air that was constantly refreshed with the scent of pines, and expelled it vigorously.

The highway appeared. Suddenly the man blurted out, "They're afraid. They're afraid of everything and everyone. They kill and destroy as much as they can."

The sunlight spread out in bloody pools.

"They're sick with fear. They're afraid of their own shadows."

Chadly was listening to the dull murmur of the wind in his ears.

"They're cursed."

The stranger's gaze was fixed on the blazing horizon. The mountains, which for quite some time had been hanging in the mist, were growing darker, taking on form again. The land enveloped the two men in its deep voice.

Chadly was still listening to the air murmuring dully, something obscure had stirred in his heart.

He stopped. The man stopped as well, his sharp gaze boring through Chadly.

"Having no future, they hate everything that does!"

The vermilion glow of the setting sun framed the outline of his face, catching upon the whiskers of his three-day beard. The light faded.

"Yeah!"

Chadly refrained from divulging his thoughts. He started walking again. He fell back into step with his companion.

The land had sunk into an immense darkness. Only the highest peaks rose above it.

Chadly was still listening closely. The regular, monotonous sound of his pant legs rubbing against each other was the only sound he could hear. The weight he bore was still firmly rooted within him; the shadows that had suddenly fallen, in which his footsteps echoed, had not delivered him from it.

Again, he saw the city he'd escaped. Blasts, gunfire, explosions, cries, everyone running, striving to save their skins. Shops closing, their windows shattered. Bullets grazing the walls, covering them with pockmarks. And everywhere, men, women, children falling. Puddles of blood dappling the pavement, darkening, evaporating; but their marks still remained.

Yet that was almost all right as long as night hadn't fallen. Invariably, at the first sign of twilight insanity returned, terror stole into the streets.

He walked on as if he no longer had a destination to reach.

The man's voice grated in the darkness.

"What makes you sick is seeing our blood being spilled for such impure blood."

"We're doing it for our country, not for blood."

Chadly felt relieved at having uttered those words.

From the shadows sprang rustling, chirring sounds, long plaints of nocturnal birds. A yearning stream of noises and wind.

He let himself drift into those blind depths, the restlessness continued within his body.

"This is it," the man declared.

Chadly didn't comprehend what the dry voice was saying.

The other said, "You're free from here on out."

There was a sort of crack in his voice.

"You can go on alone from here."

Chadly realized his guide had succeeded in his mission of getting him through the zone the military had been scouring.

"What, this is it?"

"Finished. From here on out you are *independent.*"

The voice cracked again and melted into the night.

Chadly wasn't sure when he had ceased hearing the claws of the dog clicking on the asphalt and feeling the presence of his companion.

Though he was walking through the darkest part of the night, he knew now where he was. His second night of walking; during the day he had hidden and rested . . .

Propped against the pallid sky loomed the mass of the landscape in which all lines converged. Paths came down to meet Chadly. At times, the road began to glimmer dimly, he would pivot to see if the headlights of a car weren't trailing him: that morning he'd almost been caught by a military convoy. Once turned around, nothing; there was no automobile, not a living soul. Then loneliness itself made his heart pound with anxiety.

He continued walking. His heartbeat, the wind, the silence rumbled in his ears. The face of his guide kept coming back to haunt him, then fading away. Thinking about the guide again, he admitted to himself that he'd been seized with a sort of panic at one point. The man belonged to the organization: he had been chosen by it, that was certain, and he had accomplished his mission satisfactorily. Thus Chadly told himself he wouldn't hesitate to venture out on the roads with him again if necessary. Yet the same uneasy feeling came over him again; he knew that the war had dispensed power lavishly and that it was tempting to use it even for no particular reason.

These thoughts were still drifting through his mind. He was thinking of Tnine, his village. Mentally taking stock of the inhabitants, all of whom he knew: "How many are left?" He was just about to conclude that he would know soon, when drowsiness suddenly hit him in the back of the head. From then on, as if he had been thrown back to the edge of the cliff and had lost his footing this time, he went drifting around with open eyes on a bed of waves. He rose and fell, an improbable world soaked him up; only to throw him back out immediately and recede; then return, wash over him again. The hills themselves rose and fell like vessels on the open sea searching for signs of light indicated on the maps. From a distant darkness he watched the sleeping shapes on earth, the stars; things were reeling on all sides and in the heart of the exhausted man too, who was also searching for the signs that would guide him.

Once again he tried to remember. "What village is it I'm going to?"

He fell asleep with that question, forgot it. A stumbling sound awakened him. He was dreaming of death with his eyes open. He was listening to the moaning of voices he had never heard before: voices as cruel as desire. The call, if it was in fact a call, arose at once from very near and from a great distance: from the wild entrails of the night and from an ancient house lost among a few apricot trees, a fig tree with several trunks, and some cactuses.

Suddenly, he was just a child, smelling the odors of the house, feeling the coolness of its walls, hearing the voices of its inhabitants. The door to a room was slightly ajar. Inside piles of woolen blankets, a jumble of shadows could be seen. A woman was stamping her bare feet on the floor, a flap of her tunic hitched up to her waist. She fainted as soon as he glimpsed her.

. . . While his weight pulled him down toward the roots, the stars began to buzz excitedly, shooting out blinding cries in his direction. Torn between feelings of lightness and heaviness, he no longer knew what was becoming of him. The fields, the night: what was more real about them than the sky?

The road sloped upward. He was tired. He wanted to walk on.

Walk on? To go where?

He hadn't enough strength left. He left the road, entered a meadow where he stretched out in a hollow.

He felt the gentleness of the earth.

He contemplated the stars, sent a wink their way. They all came raining down from the sky.

The incandescent shower hadn't reached his body before he was asleep.

Wake up: dawn is breaking! It's not every day that one comes back. That one comes back home. Worn pelisse, weariness has fallen from your shoulders. This is the most invigorating hour, when life takes stock of the living. Wake up! Men will soon be coming out into the fields . . .

Chadly opened his eyes to the babbling light. The blaze swelled, dazzled him.

Blinding swarms came rushing up from the depths of the horizon where the mountains were dissolving. They strayed in among the olive trees, mingled with the fragrance of thyme, of mastic, of damp earth, came to a stop. Nothing else moved in the flickering light. Then they went quietly flooding back out again.

Sunk in the slowly waxing, cold morning light, the land slept on.

Chadly stood up, gazed into the distance in the direction of his village. The hills, the trees, the crops, seemed unaware of human existence. The intensity of that beatitude, free of all memory, made him uneasy.

He stood there unable to make up his mind to resume walking. He scanned the hilltops again. The land was nothing but forgetfulness. Not a single shape of a fellah or a beast to be seen.

He thought he saw a shadow silhouetted against the light.

He rushed forward, his eyes riveted on a single spot in space. Abandoning the idea of reaching his home by circuitous paths, as he had at first intended to do in order to avoid curious inhabitants, he went charging down the main road. Soon a flock of houses appeared, huddled on a hillock. He went on at a run.

And then stopped short.

The village stood before him, cold, sullen, as austere as a casbah. Not a plume of smoke hung over the terraces. Each home stood silently against the taut sky which was turning a greenish color in the heat. Only flights of starlings pursuing one another filled the air with black wings and shrill cries.

He climbed slowly up the rest of the rocky incline. His heart echoed with the waves of blood crashing into it. He made his way up into the narrow streets. The clusters of starlings swirled up higher, fled, and it seemed as if the silence they left behind was trying to bar his way.

He walked on anyway, inspected the first house he came upon. The windows and doors had been walled up. The second one too was a blind block. He peered around at the others. Their openings had similarly disappeared, filled up with stones and mortar. A kind of night rose to blot out his senses.

He resurfaced in the boundless morning light and, with aching pupils, finished making his way around the village.

All the doors and windows had been sealed.

What about my house? The time that delayed the second part of his question was incalculable. *What has become of it?* He had already escaped the labyrinth of alleyways and was rushing onward; was about a hundred and fifty yards higher up—or how far? The path, strewn with broken rocks, was still climbing. He recognized the trees, his trees: their foliage protected the building, of which one yellow ochre corner peeked though the branches. So he had recognized them. He had counted them too. At the same instant he arrived in front of the porch.

Walled up.

He began to tremble, imperceptibly at first, then uncontrollably.

To his great stupefaction, he heard himself scream, "Yéma! Aâlia!"

Calling out to his mother, to his wife, as if they were closed up inside! As if they would answer him! Maybe even open the door for him! What had come over him? He couldn't understand why he hadn't been able to hold back those cries. Startled by the sound of his voice in the immense morning silence, he thought, "I'm forgetting myself." But the same irresistible wave returned, threw him up against the wall sealing off the entrance to his house, and he pounded on it with his fists, pounded again, and again.

The masonry remained intact. He scratched at it furiously.

Then, nails torn off, hands bleeding, he fled.

The moor greeted him.

He felt as if the countryside around him had been replaced by some other landscape. The places that had been part of his life had disappeared. Disappeared, or gone back to a world impossible to decipher. He ran down slopes. He roamed the lands where, crazed frothiness, only the olive trees shook off their torpor. They awoke, stirred slightly, then continued to stand watch. The chalky light ate at one's eyes. He wandered for a long time. Stalked his own ghost. Groped about, got lost.

He fell in the middle of a plateau, sinking into insurmountable drowsiness. In the sterile solitude, he dreamt of his house, of his wife. Like the gurgling of a spring, the echo of several people laughing rippled through him. He recalled one of the feast days in the past and a red veil fell over his eyelids. Shivers, a slight thrill, sparkling lands without substance changed to annihilation. I'm dead, someone said to himself.

The sky allowed the tenebrous core of the light to burst forth unbounded. The afternoon, ripping through the nudity of the landscape, spewed up from the darkest recesses of the slit. Chadly, helpless, was tossed about in it. Then the glare subsided. Evening came, bringing innocence back to the world. All that remained was the death of color, and the man who lay motionless, stranded in the sun-worn rocks. The man who was listening to the flood tide rising within him, rising and rumbling, saying, "The most terrifying thing will be living . . . Will be living, will be living." It might have been saying other things as well. Straining his neck, he contemplated the landscape. The fields had regained their familiar aspect; the same frothy olive trees sprawled over the land all the way out to the plain. He was simply waiting.

He didn't wait long. Slicing through the honeyed light, night came immediately.

He stood up. Drew his hands up into the sleeves of his jacket. Looked around for the road by which he had come.

He walked along studying the opacity of the earth. Far from the women he had left behind, the hilltops were stirring. Their silence, broken by the sound of his footsteps, was buzzing. Their infinite respiration was shaking the night. And new stars were making signs at him.

NAËMA DISAPPEARED

Five weeks have gone by; still no news of Naëma. Nothing. Some people think she's being detained in the Bedeau barracks. The Bedeau barracks . . . People who are incarcerated there are considered hostages: horrible things are said about them.

How can one be sure? Nothing can be known for sure, no one has ever seen anyone come back from there. Wait . . . for some news to filter through, for Naëma to be miraculously brought before the court. Wait . . . That's all they've left us . . .

I take the children out for walks, I often take them to the public square we call "the little garden," where we spend a little time in the afternoon. Autumn is reddening the greenery, mingling its yellow and rusty hues with the blue of the sky. We can't stay long. Everyone leaves the square quite early and it's dangerous to linger. Even so, the children love to play there. It's also the place where, fortunately, I can enjoy the only moments of respite I'm able to find these days. This war will be the end of us all.

But if there are some who escape, they will have learned a lot. Rahim, who is only seven years of age, has already spent three of them in war, and he looks at me with eyes that are so solemn, so filled with mute questioning they make me feel guilty and uncomfortable.

A few days ago I asked him why he was staring at me like that.

"You can't drag your feet when you throw a grenade, can you, Papa?" he answered.

I was seized with immense sadness. What could I say to him? Platitudes? They don't work anymore, not even with Rahim. Bombings, raids, ambushes, you can hear the echo of everything that's happening in his words and thoughts. I don't try to teach him to be careful, he wouldn't understand. There is already that gap between us.

Another day, not realizing what I was getting into, I asked him jokingly, "What do you think needs to be done?"

"Kill them all. Set off bombs all the time."

He had said that without the slightest hesitation, his innocent eyes fixed on me.

"You'd do that, would you?"

"Yes. Wouldn't you?"

"No," I said.

I can still see him looking at me incredulously.

At the house the tenants have become more and more discreet regarding Naëma. I try as well as I can to fill her role in the children's lives while she's in prison. The neighbor ladies relieve me of some of the chores. Sweeping the floors, cooking, washing the dishes or the clothes: they take care of all that, they would never have tolerated seeing a man doing those tasks. Sometimes they even give Bénalie, Zahya, and Rahim their dinner when I'm not home. A woman with a veil regularly brings a set sum of money—the allowance from the Front—that the neighbor ladies hand over to me. The woman has never shown her face to them and they've never been able to find out who she is. They are careful not to insist either.

The house is constantly filled with ripples of agitation. It was still dark this morning, a fragrant and crisp day was dawning, when panic-stricken whispers began running through it. Happily, it was just a false alarm. These frequent spasms of tension come to a climax especially after explosions. The tenants come in bearing news, calling out to one another, the rooms empty into the courtyard, everyone comes out to have his say. It wasn't anything like that this morning, but the day was just getting started.

In the midst of those convulsions, I think of Naëma. Not knowing where she is, what they have done with her, is torture for me. In town the disappearances, the deaths, the imprisonments are taking on such proportions that no one even counts them anymore, those that occur one day make us forget those of the day before.

Placards pasted up everywhere picture men who've been executed. Courts declare death penalties every day. Summary executions are more frequent, and every morning brings the discovery of mutilated bodies. Not daring to say so, most of the neighbors—I can read it on their faces—think Naëma will never come back.

Yesterday, two strangers accosted me in the street and asked me to stand watch in front of a tailor's shop. After they left, the tailor said, just as naturally as can be, "Yes, they left a few things here."

"What do you mean?"

He went, "Eh!"

I got it.

And that was when I realized: nowadays the only effect danger has on me is to give rise to a feeling of defiance.

This afternoon, as I was crossing the street that leads to the perpetually crowded Soc-el-Ghezel square, the device went off. At first a shudder ran through the crowd, and shouts drifted up. Two shots had just rung out, followed by an explosion. People were pushing one another, trampling one another, the square was empty in the wink of an eye.

Sprawled out, abandoned, the lone body of a man whose face could not be seen. I got out of there to avoid being picked up by the police, whose shrill whistles were already filling the air.

I took refuge in the nearest alley, in a cobbler's shop.

"Well, well, what's going on? What's new?" asked the shoemaker, surprised at my abrupt entrance.

"The only thing that's new is that a bomb just went off in Soc-el-Ghezel," I said.

I paused, somewhat out of breath.

"Ah!" he went.

His long, thin pale face lit up with a smile.

"I would have bet it was peace. I would have bet you were bringing us peace."

"Peace?" I said. "No one's ever heard of it."

I still remember that moment and the words he pronounced

very clearly. The memory is all the more clear because I hadn't finished answering him and was laughing nervously in turn at my fright when two other explosions rocked the street. This time we heard wild screams very near by, a mad gunfight blazed and quickly turned into a firestorm. Silhouettes suddenly broke and slumped over before our eyes.

The sound of machine-gun fire was drawing near. I suggested that the cobbler close his shop. Without saying a word, he locked the door and we threw ourselves on the tile floor.

I was listening to the tumult rushing into the alleyway. I don't recall being afraid. I was calm, cold; simply curious to find out what was going to happen next. The seconds passed by with numbing slowness.

Then someone was pounding at the door as if to bust it down. The cobbler wanted to open it, he shot me a questioning look. I motioned him not to move. The pounding grew louder, became more and more imperious, more and more enraged. In the end the door gave way. A soldier came in. He didn't look for long: pulling my companion up by the collar, he dragged him outside. When he'd reached the threshold, he hit him so furiously in the chest with the butt of his rifle that the shoemaker vomited a gush of blood and fell over, his face turned skyward. Seeing a loft overhead, I crawled up there and hid. But the soldier didn't come back.

I waited, lying up there in the dim light beside rolls of hides. From where I was, I could see part of the street through a crack between two boards. Dusk drifted slowly into the shop. I didn't make a move, I lay watching, breathing in the odor of leather, the minutes went by.

The turmoil had moved away. Now all that could be heard were faint rumblings rolling around in the bowels of the city.

I got up, dusted off my clothes. In going out through the half-open, bashed-in door, I had to step over the cobbler's body. The streets I walked along were oddly peaceful and deserted.

We can accept dying, but we haven't learned how to leave one another yet. At night, my thoughts, the town, the war, everything is silent. I sit up, look around myself; everything seems absurd. The children are sleeping. Those children, why? What are they doing here? Suddenly I feel the urge to get dressed and run over to the old town in spite of the curfew. After that I have a hard time getting back to sleep. I fall asleep again. My head is rolling around in an endless tidal flow.

At the first crack of dawn, I go out. Hurried people are already going about their business, bicycles weave through the crowd tinkling, street peddlers obstruct the sidewalks. At Socel-Ghezel, the only shops not open: those whose owners were killed. The bullet marks on the walls, the iron gratings torn to pieces are still there, I wasn't dreaming: the pavement is strewn with shattered window panes, broken bricks.

I reach the cobbler's shop.

Closed. I'd left it open yesterday. Today the double doors are closed with a padlock run through two eye bolts. I stand there looking at it for a minute. And the owner? What did they do with him? I go into the stores next to his, in hopes of learning something more than I already know. I can't get a word out of anyone, except that there will be no funeral. All of the bodies carted away in the night have been taken to the graveyard and buried by the authorities without informing the families. I go for a stroll.

I roam around aimlessly. I feel detached from this stark day. I need to think. Think? The gaping sky, the fuzzy light, the taste of things won't allow me to. I hang around out of doors for a long time. Everything—I soon realize—is permeated with the smell and the taste of blood.

Night. Again, a rough hand wakens me, I listen closely. From distant houses screams arise. Other cries just as terrifying spread from neighborhood to neighborhood. Shots spit out interspersed with flurries of machine-gun fire. I lie still, listening, holding my breath. Those screams of suffering and fright are coming from women and men. Then there is silence. I close my eyes. The beasts of the Apocalypse can now come and roam the earth.

The only sound to be heard is the purring of automobiles in the distance, and that too fades away.

Morning. A sky washed with methylene blue, a dazzling light; and no one goes about his business without a nagging feeling of impatience.

Tortured bodies were discovered, thrown down at the gates of the city. Approximately ten of them, three of which were women.

The war drags on; it could go on for years. No one even dreams that it might be possible to live any other way than surrounded by the permanent raging of gunfire, of explosions. Horrid rumors are being whispered everywhere. I can hardly walk down the street anymore without constantly looking over my shoulder, without being prepared to throw myself on my belly in case a grenade is thrown, a bomb detonated. Just the sight of a suspicious movement puts me on guard; I never wait for it to finish before making a getaway. Once you step out of your house, there's no guarantee you'll come back alive.

There are certain places, certain markets, certain intersections, notably the ones guarded by the CRS security police, that I've decided to avoid altogether. The same is true of the streets and alleys cordoned off with barbed wire. They're not a good place to hide when a bomb goes off: you'd be caught like a rat in a trap.

While we, with hands tied, are left at the mercy of the butchers, the real war is being waged far from here. Therefore, as our sole defense against daily terror, we have sought out disorder, the dismantlement of the institutions and laws. We have already paid too dearly to hesitate or back out now. Something has been started which is worse than war itself.

Sometimes I hope I will die in one of the innumerable bombings perpetrated each day; the blood with which we are splattered, the slaughterhouse-like stench, turn my stomach, make me loathe everything. Then suddenly, I feel so hungry for life, so thirsty to know what will come *afterward,* that I'm prepared to confront all the armies and police in the world.

How will those who escape go about living? What will the return of peace mean to them? For us, the world has lost all taste and color. How will they manage to give it a human face again?

I had only just sat down at the Café Tizaoui, a little while ago, when a patrol swooped down on us and I was herded, with my hands up, into the building along with the other customers sitting outside. Crammed in to the point of smothering, we each awaited our turn to have our IDs checked, be searched, and be put on the "griddle." The dark mouths of the machine guns promised death to whoever was careless enough to move. Without batting an eye, we stood waiting, surrounded by silence over which an odd calm had settled. I kept repeating to myself, they won't get the better of us, they won't.

The check took an hour, one hour during which each man's self-control was put to the test. And then we were turned back out into an afternoon heavy with threats. My throat was sore from having swallowed so many insults. The four thirty curfew would soon be emptying the streets; I left the café. Rather than go straight home, I preferred to take a little walk. The façades of the houses were frozen in deathly apprehension. People walked along in silence, taking careful steps. The city, huddling over itself, had assumed the nasty look it wears on its worst days.

At the end of the boulevard, the blue hills of Mansourah standing against a clear sky flung a firm promise of happiness in my face. I would have gone around the ramparts, I would have gone through the gates and . . . If it had still been possible!

My aim in taking the walk had simply been to go to the kiosk in the square around Town Hall where, being an acquaintance of the vendor, I could look through the papers without having to buy them. I read the news, which was similar to what I'd read the day before, and left. I was walking along the wrought-iron fence of the museum; I'd already reached the street corner: that's where it happened. The explosion shook the buildings around me so hard I was knocked up against a wall of air that burned my face. In that very same second, there was a deafening avalanche of glass windows, screams leapt from everyone's throats. In the square planted with plane trees, people were fleeing in all directions. I turned into the closest thoroughfare. Cries, calls, orders too, could be heard.

Bursts of machine-gun fire were sweeping the avenue and, before me, a man fell, then a woman who got tangled in her haïk.

The street froze.

With sirens shrieking, vans suddenly appeared and braked violently; paratroopers jumped out, brandishing their weapons. One of them, with icy blue eyes, motioned to me to get moving. I walked away.

But at the corner of the next street, territorial soldiers ordered me to halt. I stopped. Meeting their eyes, I decided to walk toward them. I was expecting them to fire on me any second. I was completely calm, cold, filled with contempt. "They won't have the satisfaction of humiliating the man they gun down," I thought as I forced myself to move forward. There were faces in that group that weren't unfamiliar to me, even the faces of some old schoolmates.

"Don't move!" one of them shouted.

I took a few more steps; I was gripped with a feeling of nausea. I'm not exactly sure what happened next. I was taken back to the square after having been hit in the back of the neck. I found myself in a group of other Algerians being held at gunpoint. On the pavement lay inert bodies; men who were already dead, or on the verge of dying.

One of the wounded moaned weakly at our feet, "Help me, help me . . ."

No one made the slightest move to go to his aid. In the square and in the streets leading away from it, the manhunt continued. Uniformed shapes crouching, weapons aimed, scurried after other fleeing shadows. A few suddenly threw up their hands, keeled over on their faces, and melted in with the gray ground.

Just then, a man coming out of a bar—noticing a passerby in a corner—started shouting and waving his hands around.

"There he is! He's the one who left the bomb! It's him, I saw him!"

The other looked at him, not understanding, hugging a wretched basket against his dirty black jacket whose wrinkled lapels were crossed over his chest. First several territorial soldiers ran up to him. They grabbed him under the arms. He put up no resistance. They led him over to the center of the square, where they discharged several rounds into his chest, into his abdomen. He crumpled to the ground without having let go of that lousy basket.

The informer, the owner of a bookshop, shouted, "Justice has been served!"

He was undoubtedly the one who saved us, that little man, a masonry worker judging by appearances, yet smaller in death, sprawled out there in the middle of the square, stone-cold, but now seeming to defy everyone. I couldn't take my eyes off him, couldn't free myself of his silence.

In fact, they let us go soon after that. Once the neighborhood was no longer sealed off, the inhabitants began moving around freely again: cyclers flew swiftly by, customers went into shops and others came out, a ragpicker let out his nostalgic cry, a vegetable vendor appeared pushing his cart. There was no more fear. All that remained was a faint lingering smell of blood, but it made everything feel sticky, it weighed down on your head and your heart. I continued on my way, took the street that leads up to our neighborhood.

Always that same incertitude, that same insanity. Always that same gaping chasm engulfing our existence.

This morning twenty bodies were discovered laid out in the old square. I went down there. Quite a few other people were hurrying over there too; from the houses slipped faces with feverish eyes.

Around the square, soldiers were pushing the inhabitants back, setting up blockades in every street; we couldn't go any farther. I was turning this way and that.

Just then the most astonishing procession that had ever marched the streets of our city appeared. Made up solely of women without their haïks and children, the impetuous throng moved along belting out the Liberation song at the top of their lungs. Violence, rage, pain, defiance. You couldn't tell which drove those women and barefoot children on more, pushed them out in front of the armored vehicles; a green and white flag made of torn rags tied to a stick floated over their heads. The paratroopers lined themselves up around the square: as they went by, the women knocked off their berets.

Suddenly the assault rifles rattled. I felt as if my vision were blacking out. Then we, who'd been watching them, listened to their bitter cries rising into the sky, we felt ourselves melting into that same cauldron of blood and death. I wanted to run over to them, bellow out the chant with them, and be shot.

The blast of gunfire turned toward us. Everyone scattered, trampled on one another amid shrieks, fell to their knees.

Two o'clock in the morning.

An explosion shatters the emptiness. A rumbling sound rises in the distance. Gunshots punctuate the darkness causing spasmodic rifle fire in response. Some half-tracks roll by, shaking the houses. Then nothing more. Not a sound to be heard. The silence adds more walls to the night.

Day breaks with a milky chill, light streams down by the ton; even the cicadas let themselves be drawn into it, come back to life, begin their song. Swarms of kids come tumbling out of the buildings, take possession of the street.

Today I am buoyed with a mad hope. What does it mean? A desire to survive, in spite of everything, in spite of the general collapse? I'm prepared to swear, whether anyone wants to believe me or not, that salvation, peace, victory will come tomorrow! Vibrant and firm, I straighten myself up, brace myself, encourage the others.

Meanwhile, refugees are beginning to flock in from the countryside. Starving, exhausted, along with the smell of the earth they bring with them a fearsome wind, a mute violence. I think of the calm fields surrounding the town and of the threat they conceal. Even the trees—immobile, their riotous foliage licked by invisible flames—seem to be lying in wait for something.

Yet seeing the women back in their doorways, or gathered together in the courtyard, hearing the hum of their conversations, I have the odd feeling that nothing has changed, that nothing will change. It's like this uniformly beautiful weather. Neither fog nor rain will ever come to trouble it. This weather is absolute madness!

I am still free and alive, but every day I ask myself why I deserve to be and what good it does me. Gunfire continues to break out at all hours, my thoughts turn suddenly to Naëma, then come back to the dangers each second brings. I think of her at night when, eyes open in the dark, I listen to the slightest sounds in the city, but most of all in the morning, when the children are waking up and we need her most. These bright blue mornings, almost winter mornings, are the one thing that could make life seem worth living again if it weren't that I wake up exactly as I go to bed: ridden with anxiety.

Life is a frozen nightmare—imperceptibly, the waiting turns into acceptance of the inevitable. Slowly the idea that I'll never see Naëma again, that she'll never come back, that she'll never walk around in this room again is worming its way into my mind. Yet I still go on living, I still perk up my ears to sounds and voices in the house, listen to the neighbor's stories.

After that there were several days of strong wind. Autumn died. Once its splendor swept away, gray overcast skies were finally able to settle in. The trees stiffened and, above their dried branches, dark clouds peopled the sky. Even in my despair and indifference, this turn in the weather delighted me. The last days of the season had become unbearable, what with their brightness, their transparency, their purity.

It started to rain; it was a relief. It rained for a long time. Steady, streaming, stifling rain slipping slowly over the charred land. The street warfare died down.

While I am digging up these memories, it is also raining, and it's as if it had never stopped raining since then. In the sodden, drenched city I continued to spend days and weeks going on errands, carrying out procedures, soliciting aid; I went knocking on innumerable doors trying to find my wife. It seems as if it were yesterday, it's today. It was all in vain. The rain beats down upon a fuliginous world, upon bared branches, rain-smudged houses. I look at the low, heavy sky, and the same closed sky as yesterday, the same streets drowning in mist and fog, the same phantoms of passersby loom up before my eyes. I was still buoyed with a kind of hope—a hope so limited, I must admit, so inaccessible, that today I hesitate to even call it hope. A stone had been thrown into a chasm and I was listening to its interminable fall. I was that stone; perhaps the hope I clung to was that it would never reach the bottom.

Every now and again, when a break in the rain cast a dim light on the city, I went out and roamed the streets. I tried to become interested in other people's lives, for lack of being able to muster interest in my own; in doing so, I stopped being preoccupied with myself. And one morning, quite early, someone came to ring the bell at my house.

The man waiting for me on the doorstep was a complete stranger. He drew me slightly over to one side and began talking in a low voice. He explained that since the death of a certain cobbler, there was a bit of a problem: the man's shop was in a critical location and hadn't been singled out by the police, in spite of what had happened. It could therefore be used again.

"You must have been on good terms with him," he added, "since you went and asked his neighbors what had become of him the day after the massacre. Since that day we haven't found anyone to replace him, to open the shop back up. Especially no one with whom the neighbors are familiar. Nevertheless it's crucial to open the place back up. Wouldn't you be willing to . . . Oh! You've got time to think it over, we're not rushing you! You don't even have to answer if you don't feel like it!"

I let the man make his speech, to give me time to form an opinion of him.

"Have you got the keys?" I asked when he'd finished.

From his pocket he pulled a ring holding two keys together. I took it, and he walked away.

I'll stop this reminiscing: it's the thought of my wife, of the cobbler, of the others, that has given me strength and helped me to keep on living until today. They, at least, knew what they died for.

HE WHO BESTOWS ALL WORLDLY GOODS

That old Karmoni! By now he must be driving a hard bargain with the devil for his soul. Oh yes! Even in hell, where I've no doubt he went, he must be trying to take advantage of the new, but not unexpected, situation. And he'll surely succeed one way or another . . . if he hasn't already! We can all attest to the fact that our town, which has at no time been lacking in wheeler-dealers, has never known a craftier trafficker, a more resourceful old fox than he. After having drunk up the fortune he'd made by means he was never very scrupulous about, he died. I suppose with no regrets. I mean, feeling satisfied he wasn't leaving one solid cent behind.

But there is someone who holds a grudge against him: the gravedigger, Omar Douidi, precisely the same man who dug his grave and was also one of his friends. He'll never forgive him.

Omar Douidi declares, "Every night, I hear Karmoni whimpering under the blows. Claiming his innocence. But that dirty dog will confess in the end! There are too many witnesses against him, he's made too many people unhappy!"

"Why," Moulaï Soltan was asked, "why are you and your friends always hanging around that crook Karmoni like gnats about a bowl of vinegar? What do you get out of listening to his nonsense?"

"As long as he buys us drinks, he can say whatever he likes. No one listens to him."

Karmoni was telling his regular gang the following story: "Every night, I went home drunk . . ."

I interrupt him just to remark that if someone had decided

right then to point out he hadn't changed his habits in the least, the careless fellow would have discovered the man's superior pride, and in the most unfortunate manner: he would never have been served another drink.

So, he was saying, "Every night, I went home drunk and without really knowing what I was doing, as soon as I found myself in front of an old mural clock from Mangana hanging in my room, I drew the five-thousand-franc bank notes out from the inside pocket of my jacket and stuffed them into the clock case, saying, 'Here, monster. Eat!' The same scene must have been repeated every night for a long time. But the next morning—nothing—a complete blank, it had all been erased from my mind! You can imagine, I would go home drunk . . . so drunk I wouldn't have been able to tell a cat from an elephant! Then one day my wife comes to tell me that the clock has stopped. 'The clock has stopped?' I say to her, 'It's just that it's too old! It needs some rest!' But you know how women are when they happen to get an idea into their heads. They're so surprised, they have to tell the whole world about it before they can believe it themselves. No matter how hard I tried to ignore her, she stuck to her guns and nagged me morning and night about that clock of hers. She had decided that the mechanism, which had known our ancestors, must be repaired! Finally I go to see whether there's anything I can do, just so I don't have to listen to my wife anymore. Indeed, the pendulum isn't swinging. I give the clock a kick: it remains just as still. I open the case with the weights and all the rest, to try to find out what's going on inside. And what do I see? Five-thousand-franc notes! There are so many of them, and they are so crammed in, they've blocked everything up. I call out to my wife, 'Hurry up! Bring some empty cushion covers! We'll fill them with these notes!' She comes over, takes a look, and almost faints. Then she starts crowing, 'Where have all these riches come from? . . . All these riches? God has taken us into his holy care . . . Is it *them*? Is it the spirits, who have visited our house?' She who had never raised her voice except for recriminations! My word, she was delirious!

"Suddenly, remembering what I'd done, I say, 'Silly! I'm the one who threw the bills in there when I came home drunk! I'm responsible, and no one else!'

"She looks me up and down. Says, 'Do you really want me to believe that? Oh no, it's impossible! It's *them,* it's the spirits!' And keeps giving me knowing winks. I couldn't believe it. Impossible to convince her, impossible to make her accept that I was the one behind the enigma. 'The spirits it is then!' I consented, to put an end to the discussion. We filled several cushion covers with the bills and the clock started working again."

As he was walking out to go drink with his group of devotees in a different hole-in-the-wall, using his bank notes, Karmoni wrapped up two fried fish, some snails, and some olives that had been served as appetizers.

"You, for example," he said to them one day, "you wish this war would end. But that's something that will never happen to me. You too ought to wish it would last as long as possible."

They looked at him in silence.

"Might you tell us why?" someone asked.

"Well of course! As long as it lasts, you'll be able to drink at my expense!"

It's true, he did rake in a lot of money with the war. So much so he didn't know what to do with it. He got involved in schemes that were so complicated he could make neither head nor tail of them and ended up having to rely upon his guardian angels to get him out of the mess. He was a contractor for the French army, but his vegetable trucks always carried a few crates of arms among the crates of tomatoes and squash from one city to the next. The other side was probably not unaware of these shenanigans. Maybe he gave them information in exchange. In any case, the fortune he amassed by the sackful vanished just as quickly, but not without a few handfuls falling into the laps of a number of needy in the city and providing them with food. Therefore, when his body was discovered one morning riddled with bullets, everyone was appalled. The day of his funeral was a day of grief for all. Never had such an impressively large, solemn cortege accompanied a just man to his last resting place. The French authorities delegated some officials, and military honors were paid to his remains. But some people who were in the know maintained that several top leaders from the Front were also following the casket. In the end, it became clear to everyone that the two parties present were innocent, that neither of them could have ordered the execution. There remained the possibility of its being the act of some reckless young fanatic! That seemed to be the most plausible hypothesis. In those days, it could happen at any time.

Only Omar Douidi, the gravedigger, claimed the contrary and still carried a grudge against him.

"It's the people's justice!" he declared.

One thing you need to know is that Karmoni never offered him a single drink in his life.

"What?" he would say indignantly. "You can hardly wait for the chance to bury me, and you want me to buy you a drink? You'll never get it from this hand! I'd rather have it cut off!"

When the patriots hiding out in the mountains saw one of Karmoni's trucks appear in the distance, they would clap their hands, jump up and down and shout, "*Rezak dja!* Rezak is here!"

Rezak: He who bestows all worldly goods.

THE END

Mr. Albert came hurrying up all excited.

"They're gone, sir! They've all abandoned the farm!"

He forgot to make the motions of a military salute as he usually did upon approaching his boss.

Jean Brun understood immediately: his laborers had all gone off into the mountains too, to join the *others* . . .

"What? All of them?"

"All of them!" echoed the farmhand.

Jean Brun regretted having asked that question. He had been expecting this type of thing for quite some time, he had seen the danger mounting. However, he wouldn't have thought the news would come as such a surprise to him. In truth, convinced that he was an exception, he thought neither he nor his farm would be affected by the trouble. He was deeply tied to the simple folk who were his day laborers, he felt they were his friends and believed they felt the same way about him. No, he wasn't mistaken, he couldn't be mistaken. And . . .

And he didn't know what to think, his mind was drawing a blank, he stood there petrified. A second. Then gained control of himself. "Now, now," he said to himself, "the confidence we've built up is based on years of common effort. It simply isn't possible. Years! That's the way it's always been! It isn't possible that from one day to the next . . . Unless it was all . . . it was all nothing but lies." No! Jean Brun felt like bursting out laughing, the idea seemed so ludicrous to him. But his heart immediately sank as he felt a dark, bitter breath upon it, one that was quite different from the wind whistling softly over the fields, a spring wind. Suddenly, the colonist got a glimpse of the pending disaster.

He silenced the alarms sounding in his mind. "Nothing is

lost," he said to himself. *"Nothing is lost?"* scoffed an unfamiliar voice deep within him, *"Everything is lost!"* He thought, "Here I am getting upset and scowling upon encountering the first obstacle. Don't let it get us all worked up."

The pale, hazy morning was dawning over an eerie solitude. Jean Brun examined the frostbitten countryside in which the winter had barely begun to retreat. As far as the eye could see, the land belonged to him. Nothing was moving in all that mist, all that vastness. Or in the surrounding hills either, where the grass was tough, where stubs of gray rock protruded, where the ravines were precipitous. Studded with tiny hovels, those parapets would become animated very early with the comings and goings of peasants, of donkeys the size of figurines, or herds of goats. They remained deathly still, as if they had been hastily evacuated. His gaze wandered back to his lands, lingered upon the silver of the olive trees, the brown roughness of the plowed fields. A handsome domain: clean, well-kept, as harmonious as the fingers of the hand. The wind blew in Jean Brun's hair, ruffling it. That emptiness, that unaccustomed silence, were disconcerting. The wind itself was sounding an indefinable warning. "Everything will turn out all right in the end," said Jean Brun to himself, "there's undoubtedly been some kind of misunderstanding." *"Stupid!"* retorted the other voice. *"A misunderstanding? Idiot! You'll see what's going to happen!"* He quickly silenced it. "Nothing is going to happen! None of what you are assuming. I know what I'm talking about. A single word from me, yes, just one word, and they'll come back to their work."

Without wishing to boast, he could claim to have won the hearts of his people. When it came to the well-being of his laborers and their families, money was no obstacle, and he followed the native saying "Do good and then forget about it. You will be repaid . . ."

The same mocking laughter echoed in the back of his mind. Jean Brun: "Yes, I have done much good! I was always obliging! A misunderstanding, that's all it is!" Drawing itself out, the malicious laughter made his heart sink again. *"Yet they refused to come down from their rocky dens this morning. You were a good friend of theirs, only they didn't come! You say you aren't ashamed of your feelings, but be careful."*

"I would be curious, quite curious to know how they're going to live without the work I give them. What's gotten into them? How did they get to this point?" he thought. A surge of blood washed through him, going all the way up to his brain, making him feel suddenly hot and setting his face on fire. "Obviously, I won't give in! Nothing will change! Change?" He was surprised he had even thought of that. The next minute, another surge of blood, but ice-cold this time, engulfed him, throwing open the gates to an abandoned land, a land given over to desolation. Beyond—on the other side—the voice was saying, "*We will give in! We've already given in. It's too late. Too late!*" And the vast sterile stretch disappeared, replaced by the land which belonged to him, whose sap ran under his feet, surrounded him with a living rampart.

They'll come back. They'll work. Jean Brun stared at the dark land under the frothy waves of olive trees, it seemed mute. He knew though that it was gentle and bountiful, but this wasn't the first time he'd seen its face closed. His eyes avidly searched that stillness, that depth. Suddenly it seemed as if everything in the land that had been dominated, tamed, had vanished. All that remained was this strange hostility. He imagined—God knows why—a woman being held in one's arms while at the same time she is standing at a distance, inaccessible. In truth, no words could translate what he was thinking, for, though complex, it was still simpler and more direct than any familiar words.

He allowed himself to drift off into the feeling of security that was insidiously enveloping him. This land protected him from all threats. But the threat, he answered himself with a start, comes from the land itself! It is a threat in itself! Those who don't want to come back and work of their own volition will be brought back to the tune of the whip! And be happy about it to boot! They'll march under the whip until their very last breath! He remembered the words of fat old Rémusse. He'd spoken them several months before in the Colonial House.

"We have to put everything we've got into it! Everything we've got! And we'll bring them to heel, wipe them out. We have to risk everything."

And he, Jean Brun, hadn't agreed with him, had instead tried to tone down his ardor, to reason with him. What an idiot! Now I'm afraid I've made an enemy of him. He was right, he saw more clearly than I did.

The wind too spoke in confidential tones, using rapid words, prepared long ago: "After all, they need to be given a lesson every now and again so they won't think they can get away with everything." And Gabriel Rémusse's voice echoed again in his mind, "To befriend the fellahs is to disturb the peace!" He saw the poverty-stricken condition of the people as a fatality the land carried in its loins.

"If you believe that what we are doing is reprehensible," the General had said the other day at a reception for all the colonists in the region, "all we can do is wash our hands of the matter, we'll throw in the towel, and you defend your lives and property yourselves. But if we are here to protect you, you must help us, and not only help, but also allow for punishment. It's an inevitable law. And if it is the law, then you will have to excuse me, but we are no crueler than you are. We must apply it strictly, unwaveringly, and, I repeat, to the best of our ability."

Saying those words, the man, already weighed down with age, had a gentle, pitiful, look in his eyes, a sort of distracted disillusionment. And it had again been he, Jean Brun, who had objected to taking repressive measures to calm the peasants down. "It's nothing but a flare-up, let it alone and it will go out on its own. But blow on it, and it will devastate the whole country. What you are suggesting almost amounts to setting this region ablaze." He was in the middle of pronouncing these words when he was struck by the manner in which he was expressing himself. How different he was from the General, all the way down to the manner in which he expressed himself! He had spoken as his laborers did, in analogies. The General doesn't know. He isn't aware of what can be accomplished with the native population through friendship! He will never be able to understand that. He's not from here. You can't discuss things with men who don't know this country.

That's what Jean Brun had thought at the time.

And he recalled the group of fellahs he happened upon one morning gathered around a fire burning between three large stones and toward which they were all extending their open hands. That was long ago, it was wintertime. He had stopped next to them.

"May peace be with you!"

"Salam!" they said.

"Is this all you could think of to do?" he said jokingly.

They didn't answer him. He could see their breaths smoking in the freezing air. Those men, motionless and suddenly mesmerized, were contemplating the glowing blaze pulsing like a large heart between the stones. From time to time, flashes of firelight lit up their faces and reflected in their eyes. Just then, an odd sensation of estrangement came over Jean Brun, but in the very same instant, watching the hunched, exhausted silhouettes, somewhere deep in his heart he felt a small something had been touched, changed forever. In the thick dreary fog, it was singing. Jean Brun gazed at the fields stretching deep into the distance before his eyes in the chilly winter morning and could hear nothing but its voice. The voice didn't stop even when he could no longer see his vineyards, his wheat fields, his orange groves; and yet his heart had been suddenly and unbearably engulfed in uncertainty. All that winter, the peasants, eerie and fearsome, had roamed about like phantoms come up from the depths of the frozen and silent earth.

The harsh breath of spring chafed the fields over which it endlessly swept and played in Jean Brun's hair. The beginnings of baldness had widened his forehead, and under the well-formed brow, his calm, pale blue eyes betrayed a stubborn look. The landowner was wearing the same slightly worn light gray suit he was seen in every day. Not really tall, of average height, at over fifty his features were still surprisingly youthful, especially when the fresh air had rubbed his cheekbones red like on this morning. His unbuttoned jacket was flapping in the wind; a delicate silver chain glittered across his vest. He dismissed his farmhand and simply murmured:

"What in hell has gotten into them?"

The unpleasant sound of his voice surprised even him. He walked back toward the farm, a vast home consisting of two buildings set in an L and a courtyard protected by a wall bristling with broken bottles. Set against the low sky, those rose-colored walls and the roof with rounded tiles seemed to be giving off a sort of glow. The large square courtyard was filled with the usual activity; several workers were going back and forth between the barn and the stables, from the stables to the drinking trough; indigenous servant women were bustling about. Nothing there made this day any different from the others. Nevertheless, Jean Brun stared at those women and men. He had the impression he was seeing them for the first time, and their presence seemed incongruous. Why had these particular ones stayed? Were they different from the others? Was it possible that they weren't all alike? Possible! They were acting as if they hadn't noticed his presence and were continuing their chores. Then suddenly he remembered another scene he had accidentally witnessed.

The town schoolteacher was loading his trunks onto the cart that was to take him to the railway station four kilometers away. It was thought he had said subversive things, the colonists in the region had demanded his departure. A group of fellahs who, until then, had been waiting at the edge of town came up and stood around him and his vehicle. A bit surprised, the schoolteacher interrupted his loading and, although he did not understand their language, made ready to listen to them.

Seeming very jittery, they pushed toward him an old man who hesitated and ended up saying, "You must come back."

He repeated the same words over several times, "You must come back," motioning toward the ground with his hand. "You must come back. We aren't the ones who are driving you away. Don't forget, when you are back there, in your country, we are awaiting your return."

The little old man lifted his face toward the schoolteacher, who was nodding his head in answer. He understood! With pursed lips, he stared intently at that sun-baked face, stitched with wrinkles, covered with a beard as prickly as a thistle flower.

"Don't forget that these people are your brothers!"

The fellah turned toward the others, who were listening confidently, not saying anything.

"We know that you are a brother to us and that you will come back when our enemies have bowed their heads . . . We will be awaiting your return then."

Clear light was streaming from the old man's eyes. He added, "He who teaches his neighbors spreads God's blessing."

He stepped closer, took the schoolteacher's hand and brought it earnestly to his lips.

Silence hung over the group. The other peasants stepped back and left the two men alone together.

Jean Brun did not linger in the courtyard, but went home and thought he would be well-advised to check on the firearms he had at the farm.

THE TRAVELER

Light spills down upon you, splits you open. The street rocks. It's unbearable, the fire showering down and the bubble of echoes, of screams, of voices that are at once earsplitting and faint, that are sweeping the city away, rolling it around. You repeat to yourself: It's unbearable, unbearable . . . And then it's all over, all that remains is a persistent pulsing in the air. Terraced streets, high-perched houses painted yellow, blue, green, violet; there is an air of sardonic horror about them. Why is it that one always gets the feeling that the morning lasts all day long here? Because of that sharp yet misty light? Crazily black eyes floating behind a veil drift toward you, follow you, pass you by. A tramway begins to lean into a turn. It makes a long screeching sound on its rails. European women—they walk up to you with their faces exposed. A flowerlike sensuality burns under their sleepy features. One anticipates the violent images that will appear in one's mind upon their approach. The embrace. The denouement. Then nothing. But what about them? What goes on in their minds? No way of knowing.

No way of knowing anything here.

The game cars play when you're crossing the street.

Arcades, intersections, shopwindows. Europeans in business suits, Algerians with deeply lined faces. Brush elbows without seeing one another. Either the former or the latter are not wanted here. A diagonal thoroughfare opens out onto the sea, and the harbor below hovers in an opalescent glow. Black and white ships, abandoned side by side, are stuck in the milky gray basins cluttered with other inert objects. Above, cranes twist their frail arms while the mournful voices of sirens wail. You aren't wanted here either.

You turn into a narrow street. Endless corridor that is finally intersected by another. At the corner you go into Louis's, a bistro.

Louis takes a dishcloth that is drying from the percolator, turns around.

"So?"

You walk up to the bar.

"What?"

"Everything okay?"

There's no one else there, no customers. High-heeled stools stand around the semicircle of the counter. You straddle one.

"You could say that."

"Something wrong?"

"You could say that."

"So is everything okay or not?"

Louis laughs. His fat Maltese face sinks into his jowls, his chin, his neck. He must be standing on a platform, surely he's not as tall as he seems. Behind him hisses a thin stream of steam. The nickel-plated percolator gleams. This freshly swept and washed bar filled with dusky light is a veritable sanctuary.

You welcome that feeling, as well as the idea of Louis officiating at the ceremony, with a smile.

"Hold on, is it finished?"

"Be patient, my friend, we'll let you know when it's time to step into the dance."

"Be patient, we'll let you know! We'll let you know!

"Patience," says Louis.

"Shit, all we've been doing is waiting."

"Patience."

"How long are we gonna have to wait around like this?"
Louis lifts his eyebrows. His cheeks, great pockets of clean-shaven leather, now lift all the way up to his skull.

"We'll let you know."

We don't understand each other. We'll never understand each other.

"What do you . . ."

"Are you collecting?" he asks.

"Sure. What do you expect?"

"So wait."

"Don't be such a pain in the ass."

"You're collecting, aren't you?"

"Of course I'm collecting! Would you go out and get your ass kicked for nothing?"

Louis frowns. We'll never understand each other.

"Tsk . . . Tsk . . ."

When you come right down to it, the only thing to understand about all this is pretty simple . . .

"You don't get your ass kicked when you're wog bashing," Louis says. "You've got everyone behind you. Even God! Then afterward, you get a nice little packet."

"Yeah, maybe."

"All right, so?"

"Boy, as far as being a pain in the ass goes . . ."

As he leans against the zinc counter, Louis's bald little eyes stare apathetically out into the street. A black vest on top of a white shirt is buttoned tightly over his mammillary chest.

"It's our problem, not yours. What'll you have? It's on me."

"A glass of white wine."

He heaves himself backward, bends over, picks up a liter of wine. A little higher up, between his fat hairy fingers, he grabs the stems of two small round wine glasses which he turns right side up on the counter.

"So, our country is a pain in the ass?"

"Oh here, or anywhere else, it's all the same to me. All countries are the same. It's the same everywhere."

"You're weird."

"I don't see how."

"You don't see how you're weird?"

Louis takes his eyes away from the street. He stares at you, blinking.

"I don't either. But you're weird."

The glasses are raised. The white wine in them has the deeply cold, livid color of precious stones. Gazing into it, the light congeals on a world of reflections. The section of the street seen from the door of the bistro is quivering there, reduced to the scale of a fly, black flies that are dancing in and out. It is all gulped down in one swallow, light, street, reflections, passersby, precious stone, which warms your throat.

"You're weird," Louis says.

Yeah, yeah. Louis goes back to eyeing the street, his right forearm and side propped against the counter. He's not thinking of anything, that's obvious. He rubs the dishcloth mechanically back and forth in front of himself without paying attention to what he's doing.

"And if some guy gave you money to bump me off, would you bump me off?"

"You bet."

"You're weird."

"I don't see what's weird about me."

Louis gazes out at the street blank-eyed. Women, housewives, go by carrying groceries in string bags or in their arms. To the left, people who have climbed up the stairway where the street begins walk by stiffly. There aren't many customers at this time of day.

From the back room, a guy wearing an apron sticks out his weasel-like face; then out comes the rest of his body. A two-day beard. Algerian, no doubt about that. Louis, hearing the noise he makes, turns his head without moving.

"So Saïd, how's the loubia?" asks Louis.

"All finished, Mister Louis."

You look at the wog standing there, not saying anything, as if he'd just come out for a breath of air. And, still without saying a word, he goes back into his shell.

"Would you like a loubia?" asks Louis.

"What in the heck is that?"

"You never heard of loubia?"

"I don't think so, no."

"He's never heard of it! Boiled beans with cayenne pepper, cumin . . ."

"Very little for me."

"So you never heard of it?"

"No. Foreign food doesn't really thrill me."

"You're weird."

A straight old man in a gray suit walks in, sniffling constantly. He orders a double Ricard. He adds three drops of water to it, pays up, gulps down his drink, and walks cautiously out.

"And you're not afraid he'll bump you off one of these days?"

"Who? Who are you talking about?"

"The native."

"Saïd? Are you nuts? He's like a son to me. Just like a son."

Louis shakes his head in pity.

"And the others?"

"The others?"

"The other natives."

"That's different. You're weird."

"There are things I don't understand."

"There are things you don't understand?"

"There are things I don't understand."

"You're weird: you're not from around here!"

"No, there are things I just don't get."

"You're not from around here. Just don't worry about it."

"No, there are things I just don't get."

"We understand what it's all about. That's good enough."

"I don't understand."

"You don't need to worry about it. Just do the job we want you to do, and *barca.*"

"And what?

"I said, *barca,* that's the end of it."

You go over and stand in front of the glass door—locked for the moment—which opens onto the street corner. Above the white-painted windowpanes, a mixture of carnations, roses, mimosa, and gladiolas can be seen. It's across the street, a florist's display that looks like a china cabinet, but this street is so narrow . . . An Algerian in a blouse is arranging the merchandise in tall metal cans. To the right are the stairs that lead down to the harbor.

To the left? A laundry and dry cleaning establishment set up in a basement room and lit with neon lights in the middle of the day, then the front door of a house, a butcher shop, a grocery store with double doors, a restaurant, another butcher. After that, not much can be distinguished. An unbroken wall trailing into the distance. People are walking around in the street, which isn't even three yards wide.

You go back to the counter.

"Another glass of white wine."

"So you wander around from country to country, just like that?"

Louis serves the glass of wine.

"Got no choice."

"And you go wherever they ask you to?"

"Yep."

"That's nice."

"What's nice?"

"It's nice. You've really been around!"

"It's not nice."

"You've traveled, right?"

"Yeah."

"So that's not nice?"

"No, it's not nice."

"You travel around and it's not nice?"

"It's not nice."

"Really, I would have thought it was."

"Oh, people always think a lot of things."

"How many countries have you seen?"

"Lots, I can't remember."

"You'll have stories to tell to your kids when you get old."

"I earn the bread and butter for my kids."

"Is that why you bump people off?"

"Got no choice."

"And you get to travel too."

"I go where I'm needed."

"It's lucky to travel."

"It's a pain in the ass, mostly. I don't like to travel."

"It's just to put bread and butter on the table."

"Yep."

"There a lot of work in your branch?"

"You bet there is."

"And you go wherever they ask you to?"

"Got no choice."

"So there's a lot of work, you say?"

"You could do it nonstop."

"That much?"

"Not bad."

"You must collect a big packet for each job."

"It depends. You make a living."

"And you get to travel."

"Traveling gives me a pain in the ass, that's about all it does for me."

Louis doesn't ask any more questions. He turns around, tilts his bald head to one side, takes the dishcloth drying on the percolator. He grabs a glass and starts rubbing it. After a while, the glass starts squeaking. He sets it down behind him into a sparkling row, without even looking. Taking another, he turns it in the dishcloth. The glass soon begins to squeak. He puts it down with the others. With the dishcloth wadded up in his hand, he looks out at the street.

"So there's nothing going on?"

"Nothing for the time being," says Louis, taking up another glass and turning it in the dishcloth. "You'll just have to wait."

"That's all we've been doing!"

Louis sets the glass down with the others. After that, with a damp dishcloth, he wipes up the wet circles left by the bases of the white-wine glasses. On the veined wood of the counter, the dishcloth makes wide dark streaks that turn to stripes, then fade away. He goes around the whole counter out of habit, wiping it with the dishcloth even where it's already clean. The percolator is whistling louder and louder. Louis puts the dishcloth away between the colorful labels of the cordial bottles. He picks the white dishcloth back up and starts polishing the glasses again. When the second glass has been polished, he leans on the bar with his elbows, looks out at the street. The percolator is whistling very loudly.

"Well then, if there's nothing going on, *bye-bye*."

"*Ciao!*"

Louis remains leaning on the counter—which is holding up the weight of his chest, his shoulders—wrapped in the white shirt and the black vest. A trunk man. He's not saying anything, he's tapping on the edge of the counter with his ring.

You go out.

Streets, stores, and still more streets and stores. And the harbor can be seen. The sky up above it is lighter. A tram comes waddling up from some other era; it begins to slow down long before it stops. The boulevard is seething, rumbling, belching hiccups in a brittle light, made of scales. There are a multitude of people in the streets. One wonders when these people work . . . That's the only interesting thing about a city, the crowd. You can lose yourself in it.

The harbor below is clicking like a motor that has thrown its rods. Sometimes it sounds as if the light were crackling. One always looks as if he were on vacation in this damned town.

On the opposite sidewalk, an elevator endlessly carries people down to the train station.

THE TALISMAN

I've come back home. It's not a dream, I'm back in my mountains. Hidden deep in a crevice, turning its back on the lowlands, the *dechra,* or hamlet, suddenly appears after a twist in the path. You have to leave the road and follow the goat path that climbs up from the valley bottom. At its end, you come upon a sort of archway. Once you've passed that, you feel more isolated than if you were out on the high seas. The houses: a few mud cabins and, dug out of the bedrock itself, caves blinded by a wall, those same caves which saw me come into the world and run about as a child. Everything is empty, abandoned, yet haunted by silent shadows. Eight to ten hearths, there had been no more than that here—and there wasn't room for more. As if to shield them, the silence and a vague feeling of hostility keep you from wandering very far among those cracked walls, those caved-in roofs on which tufts of grass have grown. Scattered about here and there on the ground are jars, broken bits of clay dishes, braziers with old ashes, a few spades, hoes . . . Immobile, hieratic aloes brandish their sheaves of sabers on all sides. On the steep slopes bristling with wild plants, the wind scurries and growls. It wafts along an incomprehensible but serene refrain, seems to be conversing with the wistful souls prowling about these lands. Those erring souls themselves must have drifted up from that other landscape left ajar just beyond this one, that other world guarded by a slumber of frost and dark trees.

Will my neighbors also come back? Perhaps. Who knows? The fields they had wrested patch by patch from the rocks and dwarf palms are awaiting them, scattered amid the convulsions of the mountains. And now, yet another landscape awaits them.

The path that brought me back took such curious detours that even if my entire waking and sleeping memory tried, it would be incapable of remembering the way. That's undoubtedly why today these ruins, the silence of it all, the loneliness, do not affect me. Would the journey be as long for the others? At least. In that case, I'll be the guardian of this place. I no longer need a house to shelter me, to warm me, no longer need a hearth to survive, or the fruit of the earth. I live in the air and the light, which will shine on eternally. The sun may go down every evening and come up the next day and then set again: faithful watchkeeper, my eyes will remain open the whole time. They'll remember their homes, their fields, they'll come back; and I'll not have stood watch in vain.

I'd never left our mountains before, had never even set foot on the hilltops within the circle of our vision. Then came the war. We saw the mountains themselves crawling. In all those years of combat, our part lasted two weeks, two weeks of the sword and fire. The people and livestock were decimated, scattered, and the houses destroyed. May the dead and the survivors find peace!

Night after night, accompanied by a few neighbors, I went down below the village to bring back the bodies of the peasants. We preferred to risk our lives rather than leave our people to the crows. Invisible, yet present, our fighters held fast in spite of everything. We knew they would continue the struggle even after we were gone. One time, we found my son Tayeb among those who'd been executed . . . Awaiting them, scattered amid the convulsions of the mountains, and now, yet another landscape awaits them.

. . . It began with the crashing sound of doors being busted down. Machine guns in hand, the soldiers hurried people out of their houses. We could hardly see anything; dawn had just drawn a white line across the horizon. My brother-in-law Homada, who was hesitating to go outside, was riddled with bullets on the spot. But the confusion didn't last long. Old people and young, women, children who had to be carried, we all found ourselves gathered together in the center of the dechra in no time. And in the early gray dawn, we watched our provisions of oil and figs being dumped on the ground, our blankets ripped to shreds, our livestock shot. The donkeys, chickens, dogs, that had been able to flee, howling in terror, frolicked on the slopes; the others thrashed around in the puddles of their blood.

Guns pointing at us, we were given the order to walk. We set out, some with nothing more than the shirts on their backs, and all barefooted. Our convoy had not reached the valley bottom when explosions shook the mountains. I thought of my house.

The sun was already beginning to prickle our skin when we arrived at the village.

They led us to a stone building and crowded us into a deep cellar room there. Its floor was paved with flat stones, its walls covered with scabby plaster, the room resembled an old Turkish bath—with no steam, no trickling of hot water, but washed in the same sort of half-light. The door was strangled between the thick walls. Circular vents—the only openings that allowed the daylight to filter in on us—opened wide white eyes through the vault.

We had only been there a few seconds when I began to have strange sensations. Had we been closed up in there for weeks? What about those walls which were imperceptibly closing in on us? Something in the semidarkness was spying on us. It had to be observed . . . Each pulse of my blood touched off the distant ringing of a gong, reverberating out interminably from one world to the other. I couldn't shake myself out of that grim frame of mind, I was imagining how I would look as my mortal remains were lowered into the earth. And I forgot the thing that needed to be observed.

No one raised a voice. I forced myself to lift my eyes toward the others. Either from fatigue, or from apprehension, not one of them was moving.

Then I understood—that prison would be our last vision of the world. The men who'd come from the surrounding mountains the day before to wage deathly battle with the outpost loomed before my eyes. We'd helped them, covered their retreat . . . I don't regret any of it. I don't regret having done it.

. . . Many hours later—I don't know how many—the door swung slowly open and it seemed impossible that it could still be the same day we had arrived in the place, the same day that was then showing through the crack in the door: behind it, an abyss of time had been hollowed out.

Armed guards came in, then *he:* the officer with glaucous green eyes, whom we'd often heard about. He was accompanied by four very suntanned men holding clubs. Like him, the only clothing they wore was a pair of shorts. They walked toward us and froze, awaiting his orders while the guards lined up on either side of the door. He observed us without saying a word, without making a move, then exchanged a glance with his aides.

They pounced on us.

Would human creatures have gone wild like that? Certainly not! That bunch of demons fell upon us all, struck out in all directions. Cries, prayers, calls for help, filled the room, the children wailed.

From the door, the guards took aim at us.

A frantic silence, fraught with a few muffled cries descended on our prison.

A steady voice like that of a stone idol then declared: "You have five minutes to talk. Give names, arms depots, hideouts, tell everything. Five minutes. The person who talks will be evacuated along with his family."

It was *he* who had spoken in our language. I observed him: a large straight nose, eyebrows reaching down on either side of his face, topped by a flat forehead. But his body, like that of a woman, was enveloped with softness: in the places where there is usually body hair, he had barely perceptible curly blond fuzz.

No answer came from anyone. He went out, followed by his acolytes.

purplish puddles oozed out over the floor. I cast a look at my companions, at the officer who had turned his back on us, at the guards, at the walls of our prison. Suddenly, I knew what I was looking for. At times human beings can be so presumptuous they believe they have the right to open secret doors. And all their strength gathered together is not enough to hold back the horror unleashed afterward. Death coming to close their eyes at that point would be merciful, would bring peace and liberation, if in those dark rooms death itself was not a sham. If it did not offer them up to the endless mockery of appearances! It seemed to me that was what was happening there.

The officer was coming and going, pounding the paving stones with his heels. From time to time, he lifted his hands up around his head and let them fall. There was no more moaning, tears had dried on cheeks. The guards stationed in front of the door, legs spread, had changed into earthen statues long ago. Leaving off their whimpering, even the little babies had eyes only for that man. One of them was sniffling in a corner, an old woman chided him with quick words. The child froze, staring out dully, dry-faced.

The officer let the entirety of his empty and remote gaze weigh down upon us, waiting.

That time it was Yahia whom the executioners dragged out to torture. He was one of the many anonymous volunteers who had backed up the actions of the fighters wherever necessary. As they were pulling him out, a little red-headed boy clung to him, screaming. The boy received such a blow that he went rolling several feet away and did not move again. The woman called Sadika crawled over to him, took him in her arms, hugged him to her breast.

Yahia's pleading was to no avail. The stifling smell of additional human blood flooded the room.

After a quarter of an hour, his body utterly slashed apart, Yahia's moans came only jerkily. As his sacrifice drew out, his heaving breath grew deeper, his soul was threading its way through those hoarse sighs.

Finally, as dreamers sometimes do to rid themselves of monsters, he pronounced a word and his head fell over to one side.

The officer leaned quickly over him, pushed the executioners away with his arm. Yahia remained motionless, eyes already fixed on his destination. Sweating profusely, the torturers were wiping their foreheads with the backs of their hands: they observed the dialogue between the dead man and the living one closely.

Suddenly inspired, the officer went out. He came back immediately, followed by a large woman being held up under the arms by two soldiers. Oldja, wife of the chief of the *katiba,* an armed unit of the National Liberation Front. She'd been arrested several days earlier; her dress in shreds from the neck down to the legs left her belly exposed.

She was thrown to the ground next to Yahia.

Just then the door was thrust violently open and another officer entered. When his eyes fell upon the two bodies lying side by side, he went pale. He ordered the torturers to move away in a steely voice. They hesitated, then backed away looking annoyed. It was then that—in silence—a bitter confrontation took place between the two officers. The newcomer, quivering and evidently unable to bear the sight of the sacrificer, suddenly pivoted. Jaws clenched, he pointed to the woman and ordered the soldiers to lift her. Oldja was led out of the room in front of him.

As soon as the door had closed after them, one of the executioners approached Yahia's body and, with a jab of his knife, cut his throat diagonally from the jaw down to the chest. A jet of blood spurted out, further swelling the sticky puddles on the floor. The man leapt backward.

I was the one he picked next. My uncle, a disabled veteran of the First World War, joined his hands, pointed to his amputated leg. His entreaties met with a stony face. While they were dragging me to torture, Amran, a man of God, began to recite the prayer of the dead aloud. A bullet whistled over his head and went crashing into the wall. His body was seized with a fit of trembling. He fell silent; I didn't see him again.

After that—what happened? Panic-filled sleep, into which

my consciousness melted, swept me away, engulfed me. I experienced it all, recorded the minutest details. Yet I never stopped being elsewhere, thinking of something else. How can I explain it? Buoyed by the desire to drive away the burning pain—a wildfire that was devouring me, attacking me in the most vulnerable part of my being—I was undoubtedly trying to eradicate time, the source of all suffering. On the red veil of my eyelids I examined signs, flourishes, flaming, quivering, dancing marks. Drawn in fiery lines, each symbol appeared incomplete at first, with parts missing here and there, then grew clearer. In that way, ringed shapes soon began to stand out in a line winding in on itself inside a square with invisible sides.

The spiral engraved itself deeply in my vision and remained there. I eagerly set about deciphering it. I poured all my strength into the task. To begin with, I had to undo the spiral. After some effort, I was able to spell out some letters; as for the others—from that moment on, it was getting more and more difficult—either because I had momentarily put them aside, or because they were totally incomprehensible, they remained stubbornly illegible. Who knows if they weren't simply chance patterns the likes of which nature produces in profusion?

I wasted treasures of patience trying to make them become recognizable. First I would take one of them by itself, as I had done for the first ones. Then two. But when I felt I was making progress, and as soon as I began concentrating on them, the others grew blurry, melted away! I couldn't even remember their shapes!

Giving up trying to read them letter by letter, I then studied their overall appearance, the association of terms and the structure (which I went over several times with my eyes) of the whole hieroglyph. It was then that I noticed that, by some malign design, the clear words, the words I believed I had identified, had turned upside down or were recomposed in a different way and in the end—invariably—they melted together and became one, made up of all the others! Where was such a long form to be found? Because of its winding shape, it seemed endless. Though I have not been taught all the words, far from it,

I was quickly convinced that it came from a language that was above all languages and made them, once learned, all useless! Consequently . . .

Consequently, I had the feeling I was sailing toward hospitable lands, was soon to come upon, probably not a meaning—that would continue to remain just as elusive as it had been from the beginning—but a memory, *a priceless memory,* which, remarkable as it promised to be, would shed light on the enigma. I ventured as far as I could along that unexplored route, lit with a flaming dawn. It was not easy; more than once I cried out my hatred and my disgust to the heavens, gave up my endeavor. But my eyes continued to move forward along the mysterious path.

And I glimpsed the memory.

Very long ago, I had made up a game. It consisted of engraving unknown words on objects I had carefully chosen: round stones, leaves, pieces of wood, bones. When that was done, I dispersed them, and made a wish that each would become a talisman for whoever found and kept it. One day, when I was particularly concentrated and hoping to surpass everything I had already accomplished, I composed the most powerful sentence that can be conceived of and, like the others, entrusted it to fate.

It was that sentence which was hovering before my eyes. Drifting up, perfectly unaltered, from the hidden sojourn where its unimaginable journey had taken it! And it was I who was receiving it!

My inner eye closed over that vision and I reflected upon the meaning of my adventure.

Interpreting the writing was no longer indispensable. Having established that fact brought me peace. Then I was seized with a dizzying certainty: I shared the blessing and the joy of protected beings! An auspicious fate had been watching over me! In the past I had composed my talismans without ever thinking of myself. And now it happened that I had addressed, beyond all memory, the most perfect of them all to myself! The only difficulty that remained to be tackled before I would be delivered was to understand what I owed my luck to. I concentrated on that. Throughout the course of a life, any circumstance implies an infinite chain and is a comprehensive and instantaneous expression of that chain. Likewise, a human being is both form and expression, writing inscribed upon unlimited matter, the term undifferentiated from that which exists. I am therefore made in the image of the inscriptions I reproduced as a child on my palettes of bone, of stone, of wood, of iron, probably also in the image of a single word upon them, a single letter upon them. I am inscribed upon the fabric of what exists; the fabric from which the sacrificers are drawn as well as I. True, circumstances have separated me from them: I was the letter and they the readers. But I could thank my mangled, rent, burned body. Circumstances might have been different, and made them the letter and me the reader.

Shapes risen up from a dream, silent, closed over their secret, were fluttering at the edge of a world which is no longer servile to us, but which we still stubbornly strive to overmaster. I felt I had arrived at the source, at the point—put off indefinitely—where all paths, all nostalgia, all promises meet. While I was involved in my anxious examination, day had broken upon a land in which suffering is reparation, silence word, emptiness object, question answer, painful separation reconciliation.

The sun-charred mountains roll out as far as the eye can see. They are redolent with stone and absinthe. Way out there, just above the peaks, the heat, casting a green tinge, hangs a steamy veil into which the sky is melting. Scorching breaths of wind are erring, an imperceptible chant draws out in the dazzling light.

The red aura moving along at the heart of this lethargy is watching over the land. I am helpless against the bright light it spreads at this hour of the day. Prey to light-headedness and to the flames, I become a particle of the forces that are sweeping me away. I no longer need a house to shelter me, to warm me, no longer need a hearth to subsist, or the fruit of the earth. I live in the air and the light which shines on eternally . . . Who will climb the path now, the one that winds all the way up here from the valley bottom, who will search for his house and rebuild its walls, who will light the hearth again? Who will go back out into the fields and begin to wrest the earth from the rocks and the dwarf palms? And when night falls, who will stretch out on his pallet on the floor and know the same feeling of loneliness as on the high seas? Who remembers now the silence of these far reaches, barely even peopled with the voice of the wind? Who is already imagining the other landscape guarded by a slumber of frost and dark trees over which a red aura hovers?

But now the aura, like a precious gem at rest, draws in its shimmering rays and in the night of these mountains, shines with yet a deeper light. I'll stand watch. I'll wait.

AFTERWORD

Mildred Mortimer

With the death of Mohammed Dib on May 2, 2003, Algeria lost one of its most prominent writers. Eighty-two years old at the time of his death, the writer had lived for many years in La Celle Saint Cloud, a suburb of Paris. Dib, who had spent his youth in Algeria and most of his adult life in France, passed away during "Djazaïr, une année de l'Algérie en France," a year in which France celebrated Algeria's cultural heritage with numerous cultural events, including performances, readings, and discussions of the writer's work. Thus, by coincidence, and yet quite appropriately, Dib was honored by French and Algerian writers, critics, actors, and musicians shortly before his death.[1]

The author of more than thirty works of fiction (novels, short stories, poetry, theater), it was the publication of his Algerian trilogy—*La grande maison* (The Big House) (1952), *L'incendie* (The Fire) (1954), *Le métier à tisser* (The Carpet Loom) (1957)—by the prestigious French publishing house Éditions du Seuil that first secured his place among the new generation of Algerian writers in the 1950s. This group included, among others, Mouloud Feraoun, Mouloud Mammeri, Malek Haddad, Kateb Yacine, and Assia Djebar. These new indigenous voices not only depicted the poverty, injustice, and violence that marred the colonial world in which they lived but also wrote against the Orientalist stereotypes that characterized European travel literature and the works of many *pied-noir* writers (members of the French community born on Algerian soil).[2]

When France, through military conquest, ousted the Ottoman Turks who had governed Algeria for three centuries, the French language replaced Arabic as the language of the colonial administration, and French became the language of instruction in colonial schools. The early generation of Algerian writers—including Mohammed Dib—was composed of indigenous writers who had come through the colonial system successfully. Recalling his early elementary school experience, Dib's portrayal of his French schoolteacher (his first contact with a member of the French community) through the eyes of a child reveals the social and cultural gap between the colonizer and the colonized: "His name was Mr. Souquet. I was nine years old; he was about fifty, as far as I could tell. A bogeyman with an enormous gray drooping mustache and a potbelly. He wasn't too tall. He was French. As kids, we were very scared of the French, and so we never went near them" (*Laëzza,* 170; translation mine). Yet, as Dib informs his readers, his teacher succeeds in gaining the confidence of the class by telling such funny stories at the end of each school day that he sends them home laughing. The class atmosphere becomes more comfortable and the educational experience increasingly rewarding for both the teacher and his class.

Examining texts published in French by Algerian writers from the 1950s to the present, we distinguish two periods: the era of anticolonial struggle that began with the French conquest of 1830 and culminated in the Algerian War, 1954–62, and the postcolonial period, 1962 to the present. A member of the first generation, Dib was an important literary figure in both.

The first generation of Algerian writers has often been referred to as the "Generation of 1954," named for the year the liberation struggle began. On November 1, 1954, guerrillas of the National Liberation Front (Front de Libération Nationale) attacked military installations, police posts, warehouses, communications facilities, and public utilities in various parts of the country. The war that ensued was fought in cities, villages, and remote areas throughout Algeria. Thousands of Algerian civilians lost their lives in French army *ratissages* (roundups), bombing raids, and vigilante reprisals. In addition, the war uprooted more than 2 million Algerians. Some were imprisoned; others fled across the border to Morocco and Tunisia. Algerian sources claim approximately 1.5 million war casualties, while

French officials have disputed the figure. Fought for seven long years, the war that ended in victory for the colonized and defeat for the colonizer continues to inspire Algerian writers today.[3]

During this era, Dib articulated his commitment to depicting Algerian reality. He explains:

> We (Algerian writers) attempt to faithfully depict the society that surrounds us. We are doubtlessly doing more than presenting eyewitness accounts, we are living a common drama. We are actors in this tragedy. . . . More precisely, it seems to us that a contract binds us to our people. We could call ourselves "public scribes." This is the one we turn to first. We try to grasp the structures and the particular situations. Then we turn toward the world to bear witness to this specificity, but also to note how much the specific is embedded in the universal. Men are both the same and different; we describe their differences so that you may recognize your common brotherhood. (*Témoignage Chrétien,* February 7, 1958, cited Siblot 199; translation mine)

As Algerian writers struggled to evoke this "common drama," the texts of Feraoun, Mammeri, and Dib, which were rooted in social realism, were joined by more symbolic works, beginning with Kateb's *Nedjma* (1955) and followed by Dib's *Qui se souvient de la mer* (1962) (*Who Remembers the Sea* [1985]). In both realist and symbolic texts, colonial Algeria was depicted as a world closed in on itself, with colonized subjects caught in a circle of violence directed against the colonizer and also perpetrated among themselves.[4]

In the second phase, the postcolonial era in which we live today, Algerian writers focus on unearthing the negative factors that erode contemporary Algerian society. In 1991 national elections were suspended in Algeria when the FIS (the Islamic party) won the elections and the government nullified them. In the violence that followed, a number of Algerian intellectuals, including the dramatist Abdelkader Alloula and the novelist Tahar Djaout, were assassinated by Islamic extremists who accused them of espousing Western views, writing in French, and embracing secularism. The tragic events of this period inspired Dib's third collection of short stories, *The Savage Night* (1995), and his novel, *Si Diable veut* (If the Devil Wishes) (1998).[5] In both texts, the writer condemns the senseless violence destroying the fabric of Algerian society. In his view, it betrayed the values for which the Algerian War was fought.[6]

Although contemporary Algerian writers, like their predecessors, share common ground—a focus on society's ills—they nevertheless project individual voices that often reflect personal experience. Dib's Algerian landscape, for example, has been primarily western Algeria, where he was born and raised. An examination of his corpus of works, however, reveals that although deep roots connect him to his Algerian past, his exile in France has left its mark as well. Indeed, his trajectory from Algeria to France reminds us that Algeria's literary scene today includes the literary production of immigrants and exiles living in France. They seek their identity in relation to Algeria, their cultural, historical, and geographical point of origin, as well as to France, the country they now inhabit. Finally, in postcolonial Algeria and the Algerian diaspora, descendents of the colonized not only grapple with the question first posed in the 1950s, Who am I? but, questioning their future, ask, both in Algeria and beyond its borders: Where am I going?

Mohammed Dib, the Writer

Mohammed Dib was born in Tlemcen, a city in western Algeria, on July 21, 1920. He completed his primary and secondary school education in Tlemcen and continued his university studies in Oujda, Morocco. As a young man, he tried his hand at several different professions: teacher, railroad employee, interpreter, journalist, rug and carpet designer. These professional experiences allowed him to adapt to various social milieus, a skill that would be useful within the colonial context and would also serve him well in his literary career as he sought to bring Algerians of diverse backgrounds into his texts.

The writer began his literary career as a journalist in Algeria. In 1950–51 he wrote a column on the cultural activities of the indigenous community for *Alger Républicain,* a Communist newspaper. While writing for the same paper in the late 1930s, Albert Camus published a series of articles disclosing the extreme poverty in Kabylia, a mountainous region of impoverished Amazigh (Berber) villages.[7] The hunger that Camus decried in his series of articles became a leitmotif of Dib's writings two decades later. Yet, as Fawzia Ahmad explains, the relationship of these two writers to Algeria—Camus, the *pied-noir,* and Dib, the indigenous writer—as expressed in their writings, is quite different. The critic finds that Dib's texts reveal a direct, immediate connection with the land, whereas Camus expresses a difficult embrace with Algerian soil. Defining the difference between the two writers in terms of geographical metaphors, the critic speaks of Algeria as Camus's *patrie de chair,* using a French word, *patrie,* that implies a father-son relationship, which she modifies with *chair* (flesh) to reflect his strong bonds to his mother in lieu of the absent father, who died as a French soldier during World War I. Ahmad notes that Dib, in contrast, views Algeria as his *watan,* borrowing the Arabic word to define the attachment to his homeland in terms of national bonds to a larger group ("Mohammed Dib" 102). Dib's attachment to the land and its people make him the exemplary insider, and therefore the privileged voice in the articulation of the plight of the colonized.

In 1955, while living in Algeria, Dib joined two hundred Algerians and French in signing a petition in favor of rapprochement between the two communities. Yet, relations between the two populations worsened, and he was expelled from Algeria, forced into exile. He lived in France and Morocco, traveled to Eastern Europe, and remained in France following independence. Settling permanently in France, he had an impressive literary career that spanned more than fifty years. During this period, the prolific writer published two more trilogies. His second, published in the late 1960s and early 1970s, includes *La danse du roi* (The King's Dance) (1968), *Dieu en Barbarie* (God in the Land of the Barbarians) (1970), and *Le maître de chasse* (Master of the Hunt) (1973). In this trilogy, he expresses his disillusionment with postcolonial Algeria. The next trilogy,

Les terrasses d'Orsol (Orsol's Terrasses) (1985), *Le sommeil d'Eve* (Eve's Sleep) (1989), and *Neiges de marbre* (Marble Snows) (1990)—often called the Nordic trilogy—is set in Finland, where Dib lived for a period of time. Situated far from both Algeria and France, this trilogy allows the writer to probe the meaning of exile as well as the relationship between Nordic and Mediterranean cultures.

Although Dib's initial texts were grounded in a specific geographical and temporal space, western Algeria on the eve of World War II, he always wanted his work to go beyond national frontiers. He explains:

> I write especially for Algerians and French. I want to try to have the latter understand that Algeria and its people are part of one common humanity, with, at the heart, its common problems, and to invite the former to examine themselves without feelings of inferiority; they must believe themselves to be sufficiently strong to confront certain realities. My goal, however, is to engage each and every reader. Most important is our shared humanity; the things that separate us are always secondary. (*L'Afrique littéraire et artistique,* no. 18 [August 1971], cited Siblot 199; translation mine)

With these words, Dib clearly places his writings beyond a nationalist discourse. What interests him, as Paul Siblot aptly notes, is the way in which individuals experience history "dans leur chair et leur âme," in body and soul (200).

The writer's commitment and his art were genuinely appreciated well before his death. In 1994 he was awarded the Grand Prix de la Francophonie, a prize given by the Académie Française for his literary corpus, followed by the Grand Prix de la Ville de Paris and the Prix Mallarmé in 1998. He was still writing at the time of his death; two works have appeared posthumously: *Simorgh* (2003) and *Laëzza* (2006).

Despite a distinguished literary career, however, Dib is a writer whose work has not been widely available in English.[8] C. Dickson's translation of two collections of the writer's short stories, *At the Café* (1955) and *The Talisman* (1966), provides

English-speaking readers with representative texts published during the Algerian War and in the early postindependence era. Several of the short stories deal with political events obliquely; others do so directly. In both cases, the plight of Algeria's colonized underclass at a crucial period in Algerian history is clearly articulated. In response to Gayatri Spivak's frequently quoted question, "Can the subaltern speak?" Dib provides an authentic voice.

Tracing the writer's literary trajectory, readers will note that the two novels that followed the Algerian trilogy, *Qui se souvient de la mer* (*Who Remembers the Sea*) (1962) and *Cours sur la rive sauvage* (Run on the Wild Shore) (1964), both published in the period between the collections of short stories presented here, mark a radical departure from the earlier trilogy; they reject social realism, so pronounced in his first trilogy, for a new, highly symbolic form of expression, one that introduces the fantastic. Despite the stylistic shift of these novels, both literary currents are evident in the two volumes of short stories, although social realism is more pronounced.

As we read Dib's short stories, we should be aware of the close relationship between them and the writer's novels. He explains:

> If, by reason of their underlying similarities, we consider the body of an author's novels collectively as a different, larger novel, encompassing all the others, should not his short stories also be viewed as the component parts of a novel that, consisting of various offshoots from a single tree and linked by the same underlying similarities, will, in its turn, add to the master-novel? All things considered, this is a point of view that one could adopt in reading the short stories in this collection, although each of them can stand entirely on its own and warrants being read individually. (afterword to *The Savage Night*, 189)

Reading the short stories presented here, we become aware of the multiple links within each volume, between the two collections, and finally, between the short stories and the novels. Although each work stands alone, all are connected.

With this thought in mind, I would like to call attention to Dib's earliest published short story, "L'ami" (The Friend), which appeared in the Algiers weekly *T.A.M.* in 1947. In this story, the narrator presents himself as a lonely child living in an isolated house whose "incredible height suggests a kind of square tower attached to the mountain" (177). The boy, who has neither toys nor playmates, invents an imaginary friend to compensate for his solitude. One day, a young boy appears on the terrace, only to disappear as quickly as he had come. Is he or is he not the imaginary friend who has come to visit? The narrator can only wait and hope for the boy to reappear to get his answer. This early text suggests the path the writer will take, introducing the themes of solitude and waiting that will figure prominently in his later work, as well as his later intent to blur the lines between dream and reality, thereby entering the realm of the fantastic.

At the Café

Composed of seven short stories, the first volume translated here, *At the Café,* presents a fresco of Algeria at the end of the colonial period. Dib introduces a series of protagonists—men, women, and children—who represent various walks of life. The spaces in which he situates them are public—a café, a hospital, a prison—as well as private, the homes of the wealthy ("A Fine Wedding" and "The Enchanted Heir") and the poor ("Forbidden Lands" and "The Long Wait"). By bringing readers into public and private spaces, Dib introduces them to the realm of the Algerian quotidian, and shows colonialism's effect upon the lives of the colonized.

The first short story, a text that shares its title with the name of the collection, clearly embraces social realism. Unfolding within the somber decor of a poor man's café on a cold and rainy night, it centers on a chance encounter between an unemployed Algerian who is a habitual client of the local café and a stranger who happens to stop there upon his release from prison. Until the stranger speaks, the narrator, albeit surrounded by a group of fellow Algerians in a noise-filled café, is a man profoundly alone. As the stranger's tale unfolds, we learn that hunger drove him to steal merchandise from a delivery wagon and then, in a scuffle, to inadvertently kill the driver. Arrested for the murder, he spent five years in prison before his release.

Situating the short story in a café, the writer draws us into a space that is public, transient, and, within Algerian Muslim culture, exclusively male. Indeed, the narrator uses the café as a refuge in which to linger, to wait for his wife and children to fall asleep so that he does not have to see their disappointed faces when he returns home, empty-handed because he has been unable to find employment. Within this space, he discovers that the stranger's world, although seemingly different, is surprisingly like his own. As colonial subjects, both men are trapped in a closed world.

Although the former prisoner responds to his plight with aggression and the listener with passivity, both share the same colonial present and neither can see his way to a better future. If the stranger has become enlightened to his plight through his prison experience, the narrator, in turn, gains lucidity by listening attentively to the other man's tale; he gleans his wisdom. Moreover, by sharing his tale as well as a pot of tea with the narrator, the stranger transforms this noisy, yet lonely café into a place of intimacy.

Most importantly, the stranger is able to pass on the knowledge that he, as a prisoner in a colonial jail, has acquired: "For it isn't you who are rotten, it's the world. It's like an abscess that cannot come to a head" (13); he concludes, "I realized that what had happened to me was unfair" (13). In this way, he helps his fellow Algerian gain a new perspective on the world in which they both live. This world is unjust; it must be transformed, but how? Although some readers may find that the stranger bears some resemblance to Camus's protagonist Meursault in *The Stranger*, also imprisoned in Algeria for an unintentional murder, Dib's protagonist is responding to political and economic realities; Meursault's dilemma is existential in nature.

Using the same setting, an Algerian café, and the same narrative structure, one man's story that has a profound effect upon another, "The Companion" is more somber, more violent, and deals more directly with Algeria's anticolonial struggle. In this text, Dib introduces Djeha, the trickster of Arabic folklore of the Middle East and North Africa.[9] Sometimes foolish, sometimes wise, he reveals the absurdity of life's situations, usually by feigning naïveté. Appearing in children's stories as well as in philosophical and spiritual meditations, Djeha deals with questions of social injustice and privilege as well as issues of death, human destiny, and the mysteries of life.

Djeha appears in "The Companion" as the narrator, first describing his encounter with a young Algerian who has recently returned from France, and then his experience in prison following the raid on the café where he and the young man were sharing a pot of tea. Seated in the café, the young man recounts the fate of his father, a coffee grinder, doomed to a life of toil. Recalling his father, Zoubir says: "I remember that the pestle, made entirely of black metal, was taller than I was and weighed at least forty pounds. My father had to lift it up and bring it down endlessly, without respite all day long until it broke his back" (53). The father is crushed by inhuman labor in an archaic, impoverished world. His son will die at the hands of a hate-filled European as the Algerian War begins, in November 1954. To the question the young man puts to Dheja, "Is everything really all right in our country?" (50), the answer is clearly no.

Following the raid, and his young companion's death, Djeha emerges from prison calling for rebellion: "Our brothers out there in the mountains—had they finally taken up arms against the vermin devouring us from within? But what do you think will happen now? Each day will see new freedom fighters join them!" (63). Challenged by injustice and political strife in Algeria, Djeha, the buffoon and satirist, takes on the role of political activist as he joins those who cry out for freedom. Clearly, "The Companion" is the most politically engaged of the seven texts; it serves as a link to Dib's next collection, *The Talisman,* in which the anticolonial struggle is brought into sharper focus.

Having told his readers that his short stories should be viewed as "various offshoots from a single tree," Dib connects the first collection of short stories to his early novels in two specific ways: first, by depicting the commitment to social realism that marks the trilogy; second, by including two texts, "A Fine Wedding" and "The Long Wait," that bring Omar, his mother, and his sisters, the family his readers met in the trilogy, into the collection. Reintroducing this family, he also returns to the theme of hunger, the leitmotif of the earlier trilogy. In "A Fine Wedding," Omar's mother, too proud to reveal her poverty publicly, will not let her children accept food offered by the wedding party. In "The Long Wait," their hunger is far more acute; the children face starvation when their mother, who has left them for several days, delays in returning home.

What delays her return? Dib states explicitly that the widow leaves her children for several days in order to cross the Algerian-Moroccan border to engage in contraband, buying products in Morocco that she can resell in Algeria for a profit. He only hints at the reason for her delay. Readers are to assume that in wartime, it is becoming increasingly difficult for Algerians to cross the border. Significantly, the text also reveals the family's social isolation. Neighbors taunt the children whose mother has left them rather than feed them while she is away. Within this context, the children react to their mother's absence in different ways. As each day passes, the oldest daughter grows angry, the younger girl apathetic, and Omar rebellious.

Hunger, the overarching theme of the short stories and the Algerian trilogy, is inextricably bound to the theme of waiting; hence, the title of the short story. Examples of "the long wait" are numerous in the collection. As children await their mother's return, the "little cousin" waits for death to claim her from untreated tuberculosis. Yet it is evident that the act of waiting has psychological, physical, and political implications that have an impact upon the community and the individual. Algerians barred from casting a ballot for change will rebel, as will the young boy Omar when he is unable to satisfy his hunger. Hence, the public and private places that Dib has his readers visit are the antechambers to collective political change as well as to personal transformation.

In contrast to these narratives reflecting social realities that cry out for political change, the last short story of the collection, "The Enchanted Heir," brings us into the realm of the fantastic. Tzvetan Todorov has defined the fantastic genre as comprising texts set in the "real world" that involve the possibility of a supernatural explanation. Where the natural and the supernatural coexist as hypotheses within the text, the reader is forced into a state of hesitation. If this hesitation is sustained, the text belongs to the fantastic genre (31).

In "The Enchanted Heir," reality gives way to the supernatural as a wealthy Algerian landowner, on his way home from visiting his extensive property, loses his way in a labyrinth. Here, he encounters a supernatural world of menacing rats and women with blank eyes. When he finally finds his way home, he discovers that he has become invisible to his wife and children, and comes to realize that the funeral he is watching is in fact his own.

Anchoring the narrative in the "real world" and then moving it into the supernatural, Dib dismisses economic and political realities to pose metaphysical questions concerning the meaning of life and death. Yet, as his work becomes subjective and philosophical, it becomes hermetic. In this regard, Najet Khadda calls attention to the traces of Sufism (Muslim mysticism) in his work, an element she finds all the more pronounced in the second collection of short stories in this volume, *The Talisman* (16).[10]

Dib will return to the Algerian café in 1994, with the publication of *Tlemcen ou les lieux d'écriture* (Tlemcen or Writing Spaces), a text that interweaves photographs he took in 1946 of his native Tlemcen with later reflections on these images. Recalling the opening paragraphs of "At the Café," the writer reaffirms his commitment to realism. He notes that although other places have disappeared in the past fifty years, including the Arab market destroyed by the French during the Algerian War, the café he described in detail in the short stories can still be found today (86). Hence, this photographic memoir—a mature writer's reflections on photos taken in his youth—serves as a reminder that his texts are "various offshoots from a single tree" and, when added together, form a master-novel.

The Talisman

Written in the immediate aftermath of the Algerian War, Dib's second collection of short stories deals principally with the liberation struggle. Of the nine texts that compose the collection, six focus on events of the war, showing, in effect, that Algeria's victory came at the expense of tremendous personal suffering and sacrifice. Published after two novels that abandon social realism for the fantastic, *The Talisman* appears at first to be a return to social realism, but the sense of doubt and uncertainty that infuses several of the narratives challenges one's perception of reality.

Readers familiar with Dib's novels will recall that in *Qui se souvient de la mer,* he seeks to express the horror of war without using traditional realistic elements. As the writer explains in the novel's postface, he is trying to convey the sense of nightmare, as Picasso did with his painting of *Guernica,* by re-creating a scene of carnage devoid of the realistic elements normally associated with war. Inspired by Picasso, Dib turns to science fiction to achieve this end. In the novel a calcifying plague threatens a city's population. As the city turns to stone, it becomes apparent that the only hope for salvation lies in the sea; it continues to nurture life. Shortly before the apocalyptic destruction of the city, the protagonist's wife, Nafissa, leads her family to the safety of an underground refuge. The couple survives the apocalypse, but their former world is completely destroyed.

"Naëma Disappeared" may be viewed as a preliminary sketch for the novel even though the short story appeared after the novel's publication. Although it differs from the novel by explicitly evoking the Algerian War and eschewing the realm of the fantastic, it nevertheless poses the same question: How does one survive in a crisis-torn world? In addition, it emphasizes the key role of women in the struggle to preserve life and moral values. In both the novel and the short story, a woman's actions lead the protagonist to a greater understanding of the world in which he lives.[11]

A first-person narrative, "Naëma Disappeared" describes one man's efforts to cope with the disappearance of his wife during the war. After five weeks have passed with no news of her, he admits: "I try as well as I can to fill her role in the children's lives while she's in prison. . . . Not knowing where she is, what they have done with her, is torture for me" (121). The narrator depicts a world in which his children have been robbed of their childhood, and daily life, with its raids, shootings, and bombs, has become increasingly dangerous and unpredictable: "Once you step out of your house, there's no guarantee you'll come back alive" (125). As the day presents its challenges, so does the night:

> Night. Again, a rough hand wakens me. I listen closely. From distant houses screams arise. Other cries just as terrifying spread from neighborhood to neighborhood. Shots spit out interspersed with flurries of machine-gun fire. I lie still listening, holding my breath. Those screams of suffering and fright are coming from women and men. Then there is silence. I close my eyes. The beasts of the Apocalypse can now come and roam the earth. (124)

The narrator finds himself spared from death only to record trauma and suffering. Life has become, as he notes bitterly, "a frozen nightmare" (130). Torn between the desire to live and the hope to die, he asks, "How will those who escape go about living?" (125). He finds his answer in political engagement. When asked by a member of the Algerian resistance to reopen the cobbler's shop, a drop-off post for FLN operatives, he accepts. Were he to die now, his death would not be the result of a random act of violence. He would be following his wife in sacrificing his life for the liberation struggle.

The survivor's dilemma—how to find hope in the face of painful loss—is also taken up in "The Destination." In this text, a former prisoner of the French travels home via an arduous and dangerous mountain route only to discover that his village has been evacuated, all the homes boarded up: "The places that had been part of his life had disappeared. Disappeared, or gone back to a world impossible to decipher" (118). With no way of knowing what has happened to his family, Chadly, the villager, wanders away in shock, muttering: "The most terrifying thing will be living . . . Will be living, will be living" (119).

Having put a human face on suffering, evoking the anguish of the survivors, Dib chooses to end the volume by giving the last word to those who perish. "The Talisman" enters the realm of the fantastic by reaching us from the tomb. If in "The Destination" the emotional shock of finding the village abandoned is conveyed physically, as Chadly in his grief pounds his fists against the wall sealing the entrance to his house, the situation is now reversed. The protagonist of "The Talisman" is one of the villagers rounded up, and then killed, by the French soldiers. Grounding the text in reality as the narrator describes the death of several villagers, Dib brings us into the fantastic as the narrator evokes his own demise. In his confrontation with death, the condemned man uses his imagination to escape from the real to the symbolic:

> On the red veil of my eyelids I examined signs, flourishes, flaming, quivering, dancing marks. Drawn in fiery lines, each symbol appeared incomplete at first, with parts missing here and there, then grew clearer. In that way, ringed shapes soon began to stand out in a line winding in on itself inside a square with invisible sides. (159)

In his final journey, which he describes as "sailing toward hospitable lands" (160), he recalls a game he had invented as a child. It consisted of engraving unknown words on objects—stones, leaves, wood, and bones—that became talismans. In the hope that these objects marked with magical signs would protect those who found them, he then composes the most powerful sentence he could construct. This sentence, returning "from the hidden sojourn where its unimaginable journey had taken it" (160), becomes his talisman. His final hallucinatory vision promises reconciliation:

> I felt I had arrived at the source, at the point—put off indefinitely—where all paths, all nostalgia, all promises meet. While I was involved in my anxious examination, day had broken upon a land in which suffering is reparation, silence word, emptiness object, question answer, painful separation reconciliation. (161)

Using language paradoxically, as a means to express the inexpressible, Dib draws his readers into a metaphysical reflection on the invisible world with its mysterious and magical signs. It is within this realm that his writings become more subjective, philosophical, hermetic, and, as some critics would argue, all the more powerful; they confirm his range and depth, his ability to probe beyond surface reality to find the hidden face of human experience.

Studying this collection of short stories, the critic Najet Khadda concludes that the process of "concentrating, pruning, cutting, extrapolating, and economizing descriptions" that occurs in the texts imposes a discipline that facilitates a smooth transition from didactic realism to evocative symbolism (156). In Dib's writings, however, one does not exclude the other, and, we should add, Dib is a master craftsman of both.

Algerian Francophone Literature Today . . . and Tomorrow?

Examining the work of Algerian writers, critics grapple with the question: Why write in French? For Dib, the answer was simple. He was educated in colonial Algeria in French, and went on to live most of his adult life in France. When situating his texts in Algeria, however, he introduces Arabic words with footnotes for the non-Arabic speaker.

As Dib and other Algerian writers move between two or more languages, it is important to remember that Algeria has historically been linguistically diverse. In the precolonial period, classical Arab was used in religious discourse, literary writing, political administration; it was accompanied by Arabic and Tamazigh.[12] With France's victory over Algeria in 1830, as we have noted, the French language became the language of instruction in colonial schools and replaced Arabic as an administrative language, although Arabic remained the language of religious instruction (Dobie 33).

It is not surprising that in the years following Algerian independence the Arabic language was quickly reinstated in the spheres of public administration and primary and secondary education; the intent was to counter the effect of colonial rule. Under linguistic policies initiated in the postcolonial era, Tamazigh was threatened as a result of the emphasis on Arabic, a situation that is slowly changing today. Finally, Arabic language instruction in Algeria has not brought an end to the use of French in either the government or the schools, but it has weakened French language proficiency throughout the country.

How does this linguistic transformation in Algeria affect francophone Algerian literature and its writers?[13] When Albert Memmi's *Anthologie des écrivains maghrébins d'expression française* appeared in 1964, the Tunisian writer stated in his preface that the French language would disappear from North Africa, that Maghrebian literature "of French expression" was destined to die young (19). Clearly, this has not happened. In fact, younger writers have followed Dib's generation of Algerian francophone writers. They are capable of writing in the language that, in their view, bears traces of a colonial past but is no longer the language of colonial oppression. It has become, in the view of many writers, a window on a wider world. Moreover, as part of the francophone world, they have links to the formerly colonized peoples of sub-Saharan Africa, the Caribbean, Asia, and the islands of the Pacific, as well as to the francophone population of Canada.

Dib, in the last years of his life, concluded pessimistically that the bell may soon be tolling for the literature he helped create (*Laëzza* 157). History may or may not prove him right. We can only guess what the future holds, and whether the continued use of French will favor pluralism or result in polarization.[14] Yet, Mohammed Dib's legacy will endure. As one of Algeria's most important literary figures, he will not be forgotten.

It is perhaps most fitting to conclude with an image drawn from the writer's past. In *Tlemcen ou les lieux d'écriture,* the text that interweaves photographs of 1946 with later reflections on these images, the writer remembers himself as a child, seated in the family patio at the *meïda,* the low table that served as his writing desk (69). It was there that his marvelous adventure—a voyage into the realms of the real and the imaginary—first began.

Notes

1. Readings and discussions of the writer's work took place in Paris on January 25, 2003, at the Buffon Library and on February 1 at the Valeyre Library. A presentation of Dib's *L'enfant-jazz* (readings with a musical accompaniment) took place on January 27 at the Théâtre du Rond-Point in Paris. In addition, a special issue of the literary journal *Europe* appeared in 2003 with a large section devoted to Dib. It includes two short selections of his work: his first published short story, "L'ami" (177–80), and "Le soleil des chiens" (181–86), a short story originally published in the review *Europe* in 1976. See *Europe,* hors série (2003). For an overview of the year-long events, see Weiss.

2. For an in-depth discussion of Orientalism, see Said.

3. For a detailed historical study of the Algerian War in English, see Horne; Ruedy.

4. For a further discussion of closed space, see Côte.

5. *The Savage Night* introduces several time periods: the Algerian War, the civil war of the 1990s, the civil war in Bosnia.

6. The 1990s also saw the development and expansion of Algerian women's voices as women writers spoke out against the violence perpetrated by Islamic fundamentalists. These women writers include Malika Mokeddem, Leïla Marouane, Maissa Bey, and Hafsa Zinaï-Koudil.

7. These articles were first published as "Misère de Kabylie," in *Alger Républicain,* June 5–15, 1939, and reprinted in Camus, *Essais.* During this period, the population of Kabylia was referred to either as "Berber," the general classification of indigenous North Africans, or "Kabyle," to specify the people of the region of Kabylia. The term Imazighen (singular, Amazigh), which translates as "free people" in their language, has come into current usage in the postcolonial era, replacing the term Berber, which is unfortunately linked to the French word *barbare,* a word that means "barbarian" in English.

8. Translations include *LA Trip, The Savage Night* (*La nuit sauvage*), and *Who Remembers the Sea.*

9. For further study of Djeha (also called Djoha) and his role in Dib's short stories, see Déjeux.

10. Khadda notes that the mausoleum of the Sufi mystic Abou Madyan, also called Sidi Boumediene, is in Tlemcen. Dib writes about him in *Tlemcen ou les lieux de l'écriture,* 117–22.

11. We should note that in Algerian texts written during this period, primarily by male writers, the Algerian woman frequently appeared as either a mysterious femme fatale, such as in Kateb's *Nedjma,* or as a pitiful figure broken by poverty and a rigid misogynist tradition, as in Feraoun's novels set among the Imazighen of Kabylia. Dib's depiction of woman as a healing presence marks a departure from that representation.

12. Tamazigh refers to the language of the Amazigh people. During the French colonial period and early postcolonial years, French-language texts commonly referred to Tamazigh as either the Berber or the Kabyle language, but because the perceived link between "Berber" and "barbarian" (see n. 7), some people of "Berber" descent prefer the term Amazigh for the people and Tamazigh for the language.

13. Francophone literature was initially called "literature of French expression." Both terms designate the literature of the former French colonies of Africa, Asia, and North America, as well as the critical study of this literature (Dobie 32).

14. In Algeria, Éditions Barzakh, founded by Selma Hellal and Sofiane Hadjadi, publishes works in both French and Arabic.

BIBLIOGRAPHY

Ahmad, Fawzia. "Mohammed Dib and Albert Camus's Encounters with the Algerian Landscape." In *Maghrebian Mosaic,* ed. Mildred Mortimer. Boulder: Lynne Rienner, 2001: 101–17.

———. *Patrie/Watat and Landscape in the Early Works of Albert Camus, Mouloud Feraoun and Mohammed Dib.* Lewiston, NY: E. Mellen, 2005.

Camus, Albert. *Essais.* Paris, Gallimard, 1965.

Côte, Marc. *L'Algérie ou l'espace retourné.* Paris: Flammarion, 1988.

Déjeux, Jean. "Djoha, héros de la tradition orale dans la littérature algérienne de langue française." *Annuaire de l'Afrique du Nord* 1984:27–34.

Dib, Mohammed. "L'ami." *Europe,* hors série (2003): 177–80.

———. *Au café.* Paris: Gallimard, 1955.

———. *La danse du roi.* Paris: Seuil, 1968.

———. *Dieu en Barbarie.* Paris: Seuil, 1970.

———. *La grande maison.* Paris: Seuil, 1952.

———. *L'incendie.* Paris: Seuil, 1954.

———. *Laëzza.* Paris: Albin Michel, 2006.

———. *LA Trip: A Novel in Verse.* Translated with an afterword by Paul Vangelisti. Los Angeles: Green Integer, 2003.

———. *Le maître de chasse.* Paris: Seuil, 1973.

———. *Le métier à tisser.* Paris: Seuil, 1957.

———. *Neiges de marbre.* Paris: Sindbad, 1990.

———. *Qui se souvient de la mer.* Paris: Seuil, 1962. Translated by Louis Tremaine as *Who Remembers the Sea* (Washington, DC: Three Continents Press, 1985).

———. *The Savage Night.* Translated by C. Dickson. Lincoln: University of Nebraska Press, 2001.

———. *Si Diable veut.* Paris: Albin Michel, 1998.

———. *Simorgh.* Paris: Seuil, 2003.

———. *Le sommeil d'Eve.* Paris: Sindbad, 1989.

———. *Le talisman.* Paris: Seuil, 1966.

———. *Les terrasses d'Orsol.* Paris: Sindbad, 1985.

———. *Tlemcen ou les lieux de l'écriture.* Paris: Revue Noire, 1994.

Dobie, Madeleine. "Francophone Studies and the Linguistic Diversity of the Maghreb." *Comparative Studies of South Asia, Africa and the Middle East* 23 (2003): 32–40.

Horne, Alistair. *A Savage War of Peace: Algeria, 1954–1962*. New York: Penguin, 1987.

Khadda, Najet. *Mohammed Dib: Cette intempestive voix recluse.* Aix-en-Provence: Edisud, 2003.

Memmi, Albert. *Anthologie des écrivains maghrébins d'expression française*. Paris: Présence Africaine, 1964.

Ruedy, John. *Modern Algeria: The Origins and Development of a Nation*. Bloomington: Indiana University Press, 2005.

Said, Edward. *Orientalism*. New York: Random House, 1979.

Siblot, Paul. "Entre mêmes et autres, l'oeuvre elle-même." *Europe,* hors série (2003): 194–201.

Spivak, Gayatri. "Can the Subaltern Speak? Speculations on Widow Sacrifice." *Wedge* 7/8 (Winter/Spring 1985): 120–30.

Todorov, Tzvetan. *The Fantastic: A Structural Approach to a Literary Genre*. Translated by Richard Howard. Ithaca: Cornell University Press, 1975.

Weiss, Lisa. "Une année de l'Algérie en France: Paris National Spaces Redefined." *French Review* 83 (May 2010): 1322–31.

CARAF Books

Caribbean and African Literature Translated from French

Guillaume Oyônô-Mbia and Seydou Badian
Faces of African Independence: Three Plays
TRANSLATED BY CLIVE WAKE

Olympe Bhêly-Quénum
Snares without End
TRANSLATED BY DOROTHY S. BLAIR

Bertène Juminer
The Bastards
TRANSLATED BY KEITH Q. WARNER

Tchicaya U Tam'Si
The Madman and the Medusa
TRANSLATED BY SONJA HAUSSMANN SMITH AND WILLIAM JAY SMITH

Alioum Fantouré
Tropical Circle
TRANSLATED BY DOROTHY S. BLAIR

Edouard Glissant
Caribbean Discourse: Selected Essays
TRANSLATED BY J. MICHAEL DASH

Daniel Maximin
Lone Sun
TRANSLATED BY NIDRA POLLER

Aimé Césaire
Lyric and Dramatic Poetry, 1946–82
TRANSLATED BY CLAYTON ESHLEMAN AND ANNETTE SMITH

René Depestre
The Festival of the Greasy Pole
TRANSLATED BY CARROL F. COATES

Kateb Yacine
Nedjma
TRANSLATED BY RICHARD HOWARD

Léopold Sédar Senghor
The Collected Poetry
TRANSLATED BY MELVIN DIXON

Maryse Condé
I, Tituba, Black Witch of Salem
TRANSLATED BY RICHARD PHILCOX

Assia Djebar
Women of Algiers in Their Apartment
TRANSLATED BY MARJOLIJN DE JAGER

Dany Bébel-Gisler
Leonora: The Buried Story of Guadeloupe
TRANSLATED BY ANDREA LESKES

Lilas Desquiron
Reflections of Loko Miwa
TRANSLATED BY ROBIN ORR BODKIN

Jacques Stephen Alexis
General Sun, My Brother
TRANSLATED BY CARROL F. COATES

Malika Mokeddem
Of Dreams and Assassins
TRANSLATED BY K. MELISSA MARCUS

Werewere Liking
It Shall Be of Jasper and Coral and *Love-across-a-Hundred-Lives*
TRANSLATED BY MARJOLIJN DE JAGER

Ahmadou Kourouma
Waiting for the Vote of the Wild Animals
TRANSLATED BY CARROL F. COATES

Mongo Beti
The Story of the Madman
TRANSLATED BY ELIZABETH DARNEL

Jacques Stephen Alexis
In the Flicker of an Eyelid
TRANSLATED BY CARROL F. COATES AND EDWIDGE DANTICAT

Gisèle Pineau
Exile according to Julia
TRANSLATED BY BETTY WILSON

Mouloud Feraoun
The Poor Man's Son: Menrad, Kabyle Schoolteacher
TRANSLATED BY LUCY R. MCNAIR

Abdourahman A. Waberi
The Land without Shadows
TRANSLATED BY JEANNE GARANE

Patrice Nganang
Dog Days: An Animal Chronicle
TRANSLATED BY AMY BARAM REID

Ken Bugul
The Abandoned Baobab: The Autobiography of a Senegalese Woman
TRANSLATED BY MARJOLIJN DE JAGER

Irène Assiba d'Almeida, Editor
A Rain of Words: A Bilingual Anthology of Women's Poetry in Francophone Africa
TRANSLATED BY JANIS A. MAYES

Maïssa Bey
Above All, Don't Look Back
TRANSLATED BY SENJA L. DJELOUAH

Yanick Lahens
Aunt Résia and the Spirits and Other Stories
TRANSLATED BY BETTY WILSON

Mariama Barry
The Little Peul
TRANSLATED BY CARROL F. COATES

Mohammed Dib
At the Café and *The Talisman*
TRANSLATED BY C. DICKSON

www.ingramcontent.com/pod-product-compliance
Lightning Source LLC
Chambersburg PA
CBHW020926310726
48980CB00005B/400